A quick bayonet thrust did the job

The soldier threw down his weapon and peeled back the thick canvas that hid the heavy object. He stared in astonishment. There before him was the gold and jeweled calendar—Pizarro's Calendar. Worth a fortune. He turned to confront Dan Track.

"What is your real business?" he asked.

"Surveying for oil," Track replied coolly.

The corporal struck him hard across the face. "Answer me with the truth. What are you doing with this?"

With five submachine guns pointed at him, there was little else Track could do.

Now available in the exciting series
from Gold Eagle Books

TRACK

#1 The Ninety-Nine
#2 Atrocity
#3 The Armageddon Conspiracy
#4 The Hard Way
#5 Origin of a Vendetta
#6 Certain Blood
#7 Master of D.E.A.T.H.
#8 Revenge of the Master
#9 The D.E.A.T.H. Hunters
#10 Cocaine Run
#11 The Ghost Dancers
#12 Drug Runner
#13 Amazon Gold

TRACK

Amazon Gold

PATRICK ANDREWS

A GOLD EAGLE BOOK FROM
WORLDWIDE

TORONTO • NEW YORK • LONDON • PARIS
AMSTERDAM • STOCKHOLM • HAMBURG
ATHENS • MILAN • TOKYO • SYDNEY

This book is dedicated to my kinsmen of
CLAN ROSS
Spem Successus Alit

First edition June 1986

ISBN 0-373-62013-6

Printed in Canada

PROLOGUE

Most of the young men milling about in the palace courtyard on that day in June of 1541 were hidalgos. The name, a corruption of the Spanish words *hijo de algo*, "son of something," accurately described their social position. Though certainly not of the peasantry, they did not rank high enough in the Castilian society of their day to be members of the nobility.

But the hidalgos could boast of at least some personal property of a bit of worth—even if it might only be a horse and some weapons. The common soldiers had only the arms and armor that their rich masters doled out to them. And, of course, what they had garnered in loot and plunder.

This mixed gathering of nobles, hidalgos and the soldiery in Lima, Peru, marked the end of a fierce battle that had occurred in that same courtyard. The walls of the great turreted building were scarred by cannon fire and musket balls, while the grounds, normally kept clean by a staff of Indian sweepers, were littered with the bodies of fallen combatants. All this gave mute testimony to the ferocity of the fighting that had only just ended.

The man who commanded the castle's defeated forces was more than a lesser baron of some obscure manor. He was Francisco Pizarro, a mercenary soldier who had conquered the great Inca empire through a combination of guile, ruthlessness and bravery. And this *palacio* where he now stood, vanquished and a captive, was the seat of government of Spanish-controlled Peru.

Pizarro had come to the New World from Spain as a penniless martial drifter, the illegitimate son of a wenching Spanish officer and a humble country girl. His birthright, as was true of most hidalgos, was worth nothing in the structured community of Spain. His lofty ambitions, stifled at home, could only be realized across the great ocean in the lands discovered in 1492 by the great explorer Christopher Columbus. Tales were spun of strange peoples who lived in jeweled cities perched on mountains of gold. It was a situation where the only authority and social connections a real man needed to make his fortune were those carved out by his sword hand.

Pizarro had proved his worth in this arena of richness. He'd wrested the power of state from the hands of Atahuallpa, Emperor of the Incas. Then, he had crowned the deed by executing the regent by slow strangulation—a pageant that displayed to all the transfer of power.

But Pizarro's hold on this great land was under constant threat, not from other pretenders to the Inca throne, but from ruthless men of his own ilk—Spanish adventurers and mercenaries who also sought those opportunities that were available to strong, determined men.

On that cool day of June 26, 1541, it had all ended for Pizarro. Defeated and humbled by the vengeful followers of Diego de Almagro, a fellow conquistador who had been murdered by Pizarro's own half brother, Pizarro knew his last moments were fast approaching.

Now it was Francisco Pizarro himself, captive and chained in the courtyard of his own palace, who was to suffer a slow death at the hands of his enemies.

Among the spectators was a twenty-two-year-old subaltern named Don Rodolfo Pueblo. This hidalgo, however, was not interested in watching the old man die. His attention was riveted elsewhere. With everyone's eyes on Pizarro, he eased back into the crowd, slipped away and stole into the hallways of the palace. Rushing up a flight of stairs, he turned down another, narrower corridor and went to the door at the end.

He opened it and stepped into what appeared to be a chapel. Such places of worship were common in the *palacios* of the Spanish freebooters. Here, between missions to plunder and murder the native populations, they said their daily prayers and received absolution for their sins from their personal confessors.

But the young adventurer had no interest in confessing past transgressions to cleanse his soul.

Pueblo went to the altar and roughly kicked it aside. Behind it, wrapped in thick velvet, was a round object. Struggling, he picked it up and carried it across the small chamber to set it down on the single pew. He threw aside one corner of the covering.

The disk hidden there, bearing the designs and inscriptions of the Inca calendar, was pure gold. Six rubies and six emeralds, each half the size of a man's fist, marked the twelve months. Smaller stones showed the three ten-day weeks of each month that made up the Inca year of three hundred and sixty days. Here was the fortune Pueblo had come across the dangerous ocean-sea to find.

A voice, cold and threatening in tone, broke into his excited reverie.

"Are you forgetting our bargain, *Alférez* Pueblo?"

Pueblo's eyes snapped up, and he looked into the rugged, bearded countenance of Pablo Huevez, a common soldier some ten years older than he. Pueblo shrugged. "Of course not, Huevez. I was merely making sure the object truly existed and was not some figment created by a barracks-room storyteller."

Huevez, the same height as Pueblo but carrying twenty more pounds of weight in solid muscle, strode boldly into the room. "There was no soldier-talk about this thing," he said. "I discovered it during a tour of guard here. And I told no one."

"Except me," Pueblo reminded him.

"*Por su puesto*—of course," Huevez said. "A hidalgo can move about freely. His baggage is never searched. A plain soldier like me would attract too much attention with an extra load on his back." He walked up to the calendar and hefted it with a great deal of effort. "*¡Ay Dios de mi alma!* It's heavy. So you also needed me to—" His eyes widened in astonishment and he started to snarl an oath.

Pueblo withdrew his rapier from the man's body and stabbed three more times, the razorlike blade of the sword slicing closer to death with each stroke.

Huevez toppled forward onto the pew, then rolled off to the floor leaving the calendar intact. Pueblo slipped the sword back into its scabbard and rewrapped the priceless object. This fortune he had no intention of sharing with anyone.

A rather slim young man, Pueblo would have been unable to carry the jewel-encrusted slab of gold far under normal circumstances, but desperation and exaltation doubled his normal strength.

Pueblo went back down the hall. His horse and a spare mule awaited him below in the courtyard. No one would think to examine his load closely during the next few hours. The young conquistador planned to hide the calendar. Then, at his leisure, he would form a scheme to get it out of New Spain and back to his native province of Navarra.

Pueblo stopped at the head of the stairs to adjust the heavy load in his arms. He was so busy with the difficult task that he failed to perceive the two Indians steal up behind him in the gloomy light. A heavy Inca war club slammed into Pueblo's head just above the neck. The skull split, letting brains and blood spurt out onto the hall.

The second Indian, companion to the one who had bludgeoned the young Spaniard, pulled the calendar from the dead man's arms an instant before he collapsed and tumbled down the stone steps to the next landing.

The Indians, who had been palace servants, didn't waste time watching the conquistador's final moments. They took the calendar, an object most revered and sacred in their beliefs, and rushed back toward the chapel.

A hidden door, skillfully engineered into the wall, was located behind the altar. It had been ordered by Pizarro as a secret escape route.

He had obviously not had the opportunity to use it.

But the two Inca servants had known of it, and they had hidden the calendar in the chapel to await the right moment to steal away with it and to hide the sacred object where no white man would ever see it for all eternity.

A group of the Inca elite had retreated out of the cities. Nearly crazed by superstitious fears of the white men, they knew of no way to effectively fight them. A belief sprang up among the priests that their gods would let them know how to defeat the Spaniards when the time was right.

These fugitive Indians traveled across the mountains and down into the jungle on the other side. There, with as many of their religious icons as they had been able to sneak away, they prayed for deliverance from the yoke of the Spanish oppressors.

The two Incas took the calendar over the wall of the palace and into the narrow, winding streets of the city. It stayed hidden in a small house for several months before it was finally slipped among cargo loaded onto the backs of sturdy llamas.

Then it was taken away from the hated Europeans. The sacred object went on a long, difficult journey up into the great Andes Mountains, and down the other side to the Ucayali River. Transferred to waiting boats, it was rafted for hundreds of leagues deeper into the green hell of the jungle to a place where the smaller river joined the mighty Amazon.

This was to be its final resting place, safe from infidels and foreigners. Here it was to be preserved for an eternity.

But, a bit under four and a half centuries later, it was to resurface.

1

The taxi, with the driver leaning on the horn, turned off the highway leading south from Peru's international airport in Lima onto Buenavidas Avenue and headed toward the center of the city.

The three passengers in the back of the cab seemed an odd mixture. The large, muscular black man with shaved head and brutal face would have gone unnoticed in a group of professional football linebackers. Yet his eyes were lively and friendly, showing a high intelligence. He was stylishly dressed in a contemporary-cut Italian suit, and his mannerisms declared him to be a well-educated and cultured twentieth-century man of the world. A native of Nigeria, his name was Hodari Zulu. Despite being an Oxford graduate with an interest in archaeology, he earned his money in a particularly dangerous—but well-paying—manner with his two companions.

Opposite him, on the left side, and immensely enjoying the exotic sights, was a man in his mid-twenties named George Beegh. An American kid with clean-cut good looks, he had an unbounded enthusiasm and physical courage that had served both himself and his partners on more than one dangerous occasion. Like Zulu, George had a creative and literate side, too. He earned extra money in addition to his regular, quite ample salary, by writing articles for various gun magazines.

Even the most casual of observers would have deduced that the man between those two, who was quiet to the point of being morose, was their leader. He was, in fact, George's uncle, Dan Track, head of a loosely organized team known to their few confidants as Track and Company.

Tall and athletic, he had light brown hair razored short, and a carefully tended mustache. His face was expressionless as his blue eyes stared straight ahead through the dirty windshield of the taxi.

"Damn!" George suddenly exclaimed. "Look there. A llama!" He pronounced the animal's name in the Anglo manner.

"Quite interesting," Zulu said. "But, if you'll allow me, George, the animal is called a *yah-mah* not *lah-mah*."

"No shit?"

Zulu smiled. "No shit, indeed. In the Spanish language double 'Ls' are pronounced as English 'Ys.'"

Dan Track looked over at the big black man. "Do you speak Spanish, Zulu?"

"I don't claim fluency, Dan," Zulu answered, "but I have a rather good working knowledge of the idiom."

"Then tell that fucking driver to lay off that fucking horn or I'm gonna break his fucking neck!" Track said irritably.

"I'll be a bit more diplomatic than that," Zulu said. He leaned forward and tapped the cabbie's shoulder. *"Perdóneme, señor. Favor de no tocar el claxon. Mi amigo tiene un muy mal dolor de la cabeza."*

The driver waved back at them in the mirror. *"¿Cómo no, señor? Con mucho gusto."* He took his hand off the horn.

"Muchas gracias," Zulu said thanking him. He turned to Dan Track. "I asked him to let up because you had a headache."

Track glowered at the cabbie and fell back into his somber reverie.

His life at that particular moment had a hole in it, marking the absence of Desiree Goth. She was the only woman that Dan Track ever would—or could—love. Their relationship had been as stormy as it was passionate, as argumentative as it was affectionate, yet both knew they loved each other deeply.

Their intimacy had gone beyond that of other couples. Besides cohabiting and making love, they had faced danger as comrades in arms in such exotic places as the African continent and the Soviet Union. The last time, only a few weeks previously, had been on the Spanish Main in the West Indies.

This last adventure had ended with her sudden and completely unexpected disappearance. They'd been having trouble that went far beyond that of normal disagreements between lovers. A strong, undeniable friction that neither of them could explain had built up slowly and steadily between them. It had been soothed somewhat by sessions in bed, but it had finally escalated to what eventually proved to be inevitable—their breakup.

Track could understand Desiree's dilemma. She was a woman who was used to taking care of herself without the complication of sentimental attachments. Desiree found her love for Dan Track unsettling to the point of emotional torture. The woman in her demanded that she be always supportive of him, yet the fighter that also dwelt in that beautiful body wanted to be free of the smothering entanglement that loving Dan Track brought into her life.

Back in Jamaica, when he'd first found she'd left him, he had been damned good and pissed. An evening of knocking back his favorite drink—Seagrams Seven on the rocks—and talking with his good friend Sir Abner Chesterton had soothed his anger. The real hurt had settled in afterward.

He empathized with Desiree and, when he was being completely truthful with himself, he didn't blame her one bit for seeking freedom from a demanding lover.

And, he admitted to himself, he was certainly that.

Determined to rid himself of his own misgivings and uncertainties, he'd wasted no time in returning to the States.

But a short stay at his ranch in New Mexico, which included a couple of three-day hunting trips with his nephew, George, and friend, Zulu, had not lightened his mood.

When Sir Abner had given them their new work assignment from The Consortium—an organization of insurance companies that kept them on retainer—the trio had headed back into their dangerous world of work with deep feelings of relief. The recoil of an automatic pistol and the roaring belch of a SPAS-12 assault rifle did wonders in knocking the cobwebs from a man's mind.

When they'd left on this latest assignment, Track had finally found some real emotional easement during a stopover in Las Vegas. A cocktail waitress at Caesar's Palace had taken notice of the handsome stranger sitting alone at the table.

After serving him his third Seagrams, she'd felt bold enough to remark, "Looks like you and I have the same problem."

Track gave her scanty toga costume a good look. She was blond and leggy, and the short garment, pulled in tight around firm, protruding breasts, highlighted her beauty. He took his drink. "What makes you think I have a problem? And, if I do, why would it be the same as yours?"

She smiled sadly at him. "I've been working lounges for more than a couple of years. I know all the different types of drinkers. You're a 'lost-love' drinker."

Track grinned a little and nodded his head. "Bingo."

"I'm in the same boat," she said. "I get off work in an hour. Mind if I join you here? Maybe a couple of dumpees could comfort each other."

"Why not?" Track said. He was sincerely pleased to have her company. He tossed back the drink. "In the meantime, bring me another."

"The customer is always right."

A little more than an hour later they were together at a table off to one side of the bar. Track learned her name was Glenda, and she told him of her own lost love.

He was an aerospace engineer from San Diego named Gene who had a penchant for gambling and fast women. It was a classic story. Her emotional frailty was constantly being stepped on by Gene's cavalier and adventurous spirit.

Glenda sighed. "His visits to me always end the same. Dinner at Denny's and a fast farewell kiss. Then it's back to his exciting world of aerospace."

Track couldn't give her the whole truth of his own romance. It's never a good idea to discuss gunrunning, sinking dope smugglers' boats and blowing away certain individuals in situations that could best be described as extralegal. But he did tell her of Desiree's drives and ambitions for independence, and how they conflicted with the natural desires she felt for him—her man.

Even without the full story, Glenda understood. She expressed that understanding well, even managing to comfort Track somehow, as she explained how a woman's emotions in the modern world can rip her soul apart, making her abandon the very thing she wants more than anything to keep.

Dan Track and Glenda parted as friends that night. There was nothing sexual about their relationship. They were just two sad people talking together, knowing that in all probability they would never meet again.

Then, that same night, Track got most of it out of his system. He ended up back in his room quite drunk. Using the services of an all-knowing bellboy, he sent for one of the beautiful call girls that Las Vegas is famous for.

The woman was no disappointment. A brunette with hazel eyes and a body firmed by aerobics and bronzed by the sun, she'd given herself to Track until his seemingly insatiable lust began to wear down even a professional.

She sent for reinforcements.

It cost Track plenty, but it was worth it. By the time the early-morning sun was shining down on the persistent gamblers on the strip, he was sober and satisfied—physically. And somewhere in that glamorous city three whores, bruised but smiling, slept exhausted and wrung out.

Now, in the Peruvian cab traveling along one of Lima's busiest avenues, he felt better, but he was still edgy and could become easily irritated.

Zulu suddenly pointed out the window. "There it is."

His friends looked at a large building located near the Palacio de Gobierno. Three stories high, made of granite, it was old but stately. The sign on it, chiseled into stone above the double doorway on the front, proclaimed EL MUSEO NACIONAL DE LA REPUBLICA DE PERU.

George Beegh's lips moved as he silently read the words. He looked at Zulu. "Does that mean what I think it means?"

"If you think it says 'The National Museum of the Republic of Peru,' then you're right," Zulu said.

George grinned. "That's exactly what I figured."

"Okay, genius," Track said impatiently. "Let's get out. We've got business in there." He followed Zulu out the door on his side. He pulled out a freshly exchanged wad of Peruvian sols and threw them through the window at the driver. "If I catch another ride with you, and you play that goddamned horn again, I'll break your jaw."

The driver, not really understanding, looked at Zulu with a worried expression as he got out out of the cab and went around to the trunk. *"¿Qué me dicho el señor?"*

"Dicho a usted qué el respecta mucha su habilidad de manejar su taxi," Zulu said with a friendly smile.

The driver displayed a gap-toothed grin. *"¡Muchas gracias!"* he said as he pulled their baggage out and set it down on the curb. He waved happily at Track, then got back into the taxi and drove away.

"What was that all about?" Track asked.

"I told him you respected his ability to drive his taxi," Zulu said.

"Don't worry, Dan," George said. "You can always break the next cabby's jaw, huh?"

Track lightened up a little. "I'm not good company, am I?"

"Well," George said, "you're a bit more cheerful than a starving tiger."

"Let's get to business," Track said, giving his nephew a friendly cuff on the shoulder. He winked at Zulu. "I appreciate your diplomacy, my friend."

"You're entirely welcome, Dan, old chap."

The three, carrying their bags, ascended the eroded concrete steps and passed through the entrance. A rather fat guard, perusing a newspaper at a battered desk and wearing an ill-fitting uniform, glanced up at them without interest.

"We're here to see Dr. Cordoba," Track said.

"Eh?"

"We're here to see—" Track nudged Zulu.

"Queremos visitar con el Dr. Cordoba."

The guard pointed down the hall leading away from the exhibition area, then turned his attention back to his reading.

Track took time to look inside the larger room. He could see banks of glass cases displaying interesting relics. One, containing some old, rusted and restored Spanish armor complete with a helmet and side arms, caught his attention. He walked over to it with Zulu and George following.

"Imagine going into combat dressed in that," Track commented.

"Jesus!" George exclaimed, examining the exhibit more closely. "They must've been little guys."

"People were much smaller in those days," Zulu said. "The average conquistador was probably not much more than five and a half feet tall."

"If I remember my history correctly, they were mean little shits," George said.

"The Spaniards were badasses," Track said, delivering it as a sincere compliment. "They came across wild oceans in crude ships and forged out an empire, leaving their religion and language stamped permanently wherever they marched."

"Indeed," Zulu agreed. "Remember our taxi driver. It's obvious he had much Indian blood. Yet, in order to communicate with him, I had to use Spanish."

George looked around the chamber. "Looks like Indian stuff here, too."

"Inca," Zulu said. "We are standing in what was once their empire, my young friend."

"Yeah," George said with a laugh. "Until some little short Spanish mercs came over and kicked some ass."

"Maybe so," Zulu conceded. "But the Incas were no pantywaists themselves."

"I'd like to spend some time here," Track said. He glanced at his watch. "But we have an appointment with Dr. Cordoba. Let's get on with it."

As they walked out of the exhibit hall, George took a backward glance. "Yeah, I think you're right, Zulu. There were a lot of real hard types around here at one time."

"There still are," Zulu assured him.

"And we'll be running into a few of them," Track promised.

2

Track and Company stood in front of a nondescript door that gave every impression of opening into a shabby room.

The glass window in it was frosted with dirt. A faded, hand-lettered sign on it proclaimed it as the entrance to the office of Dr. Hector Cordoba.

The flimsy portal rattled under Track's sturdy rapping.

"¿Quién es?" a voice called out.

Zulu, with his understanding of the Spanish language, responded to the question. "We are from The Consortium."

A moment later the door opened and a short Latin American with a thick black mustache looked out at them. His face displayed a friendly grin. "Ah! Señor Track, no?"

Track did not smile back. "Señor Track, yes."

"Please come into my office," he invited. "I am Hector Cordoba at your service."

They stepped inside and found that the room was not only shabby, but was also very cluttered. The trio set their bags down, and Track introduced Zulu and George. "We understand our crate preceded us."

"Yes, of course," Dr. Cordoba said. He pointed to the corner. "It is labeled as museum relics and went through Peruvian customs without the usual inspection."

Dr. Cordoba indicated a shelf with miscellaneous items strewed along it. "There is a hammer there if you care to open the box."

"Thank you," Track said. He motioned to George. "Would you care to do the honors?"

"My pleasure," George said agreeably. He went to the task without hesitation. When the lid was pried open, he announced, "Everything's in order." He held up each item as he called it out. "One each Colt AR-15 9-millimeter rifle, one each Uzi submachine gun and a Franchi SPAS-12 shotgun complete with folding stock."

Track and Zulu joined him. They could also see the three Beretta 9-millimeter pistols, shoulder holsters and various boxes of ammunition and magazines fitted to each of the particular weapons.

"Everything is in apple-pie order," Track said.

"Excellent," Cordoba said. He went to a telephone on his untidy desk. "I shall ring up Señor Zindel and let him know you are here."

"Thank you," Track said. Although he didn't know the man, he recognized the name as the one given him in the mission briefing by Sir Abner Chesterton.

They waited the few moments necessary for the call. When Cordoba hung up, he said, "He will be here shortly."

Zulu settled down in a badly worn overstuffed chair nearby. "We were fascinated by your displays, Dr. Cordoba."

"I'm so very glad you appreciated them," Cordoba said, pleased. "I fear our funding is not on a par with most national museums, and I'm forced to cut administrative and cosmetic costs in order to maintain the highest possible quality of exhibits."

"At any rate," Zulu said, "it was fascinating."

"May I offer you some coffee?" Cordoba asked. "I had just put on some water when you knocked."

"Are you speaking of thick South American *café*?" Zulu asked in anticipation of a gourmet's brew.

"Instant Maxwell House," Cordoba said.

"As long as it's full of caffeine," Track said.

Dr. Cordoba prepared four cups. "You might find it interesting to know that the object you are to retrieve is worth more than all our exhibits combined." He stopped and became thoughtful for a moment. "As a matter of fact," he added, "it is probably worth more than this entire city."

"That's the reason the venture is insured, and why we've been sent in to guarantee a successful recovery."

"It still sounds a lot for a calendar," George remarked, taking his coffee, "even if it is made out of gold."

"Then you are aware of what it is?" Cordoba asked.

"Only that it is an ancient Inca calendar," Track said.

Cordoba nodded. "It has a combination of aesthetic, monetary and historical value. But I shall let Señor Zindel explain the whole setup to you."

"I understand this is to end up at the Smithsonian in Washington," Track said. "If it's so valuable, why not keep it here?"

"We are only loaning it to the good people at the Smithsonian," Cordoba said. "In exchange for fifteen years of studying and exhibiting the calendar, they are going to pay us a tremendous amount of money. It is more than the government can give our museum. Thus, we shall be able to make certain improvements around here and eventually be able to boast of having one of the finest Inca displays in the entire world."

"Most interesting," Zulu said. "I shall certainly want to visit here when the exhibition is completed."

"Yes," Track agreed, "but where do we come in? I don't understand why we have been chosen to retrieve the calendar."

"It is insured by a member company of The Consortium," Cordoba said.

"I understand that," Track said. "But what is so special about the calendar—aside from its value—that we have to fetch the damned thing?"

"I hesitate to speak pessimistically, but I am afraid there is a certain element of risk involved," Cordoba said, taking a sip of his coffee. "You gentlemen have a long and dangerous journey ahead of you."

Track came straight to the point. "Is what we're doing illegal?"

Cordoba chose his words carefully. "I can explain it best by saying that the Peruvian government is not aware of this undertaking."

"Why not?" Track asked.

"There is much corruption, I fear," Cordoba said. "Certain officials might even go so far as to steal Pizarro's calendar for their own gain."

"Which means they would kill anybody who might have it in his possession," Track remarked dryly.

George Beegh started to toss off one of his usual flippant remarks, but he was preempted by the door suddenly opening. A middle-aged, portly man with gray hair stepped into the room. He nodded to Cordoba, then looked at the three strangers. "Who is Mr. Track, please?"

Track remained motionless. It was Zulu who spoke. "Who is looking for him?"

"Excuse me," the man said. "I am Horace Zindel. I represent The Consortium."

Again Track went through a round of introductions. And he was growing impatient. "We'd like to get the nitty-gritty of what we're to do," he said. "And get on with it."

"Of course, Mr. Track," Zindel said. "I'm afraid we're going to have to ask you to do a bit of traveling. First by train from Lima to the small city of Iquitos. This involves a rather tedious journey across the Andes."

"Sounds interesting to me," George Beegh said agreeably.

"Oatmeal sounds interesting to you," Track snapped.

"Jeez!" George complained. "You're really charming, aren't you?"

"Cut the chatter and let Zindel fill us in," Track said.

"Very well," Zindel said uneasily. "At Iquitos you will board a river steamer and head up the Amazon River."

"To where?" Track asked.

"I have no specific information on that," Zindel said. "You will be contacted by someone who can take you directly to Pizarro's calendar."

"I don't completely understand why the contact doesn't bring it out himself," Track said.

"He would prefer to," Zindel said. "He fears he will compromise his source. Which is exactly what we wish to happen."

"So, in addition to lugging the thing back, we also have to make our contact's source."

"Yes, Mr. Track."

Zulu, his curiosity piqued by the historical object, leaned forward in his chair. "How will we know this person, Mr. Zindel?"

"He will say, 'The Inca sun shines always.' You will reply, 'As long as its people live.'"

"Okay," Track conceded. "I appreciate the care and planning. But I'd really like to know more about how we'll be bringing this thing out. Hell, it must weigh a ton."

"It is estimated at approximately 150 pounds," Zindel said.

"It'll take the three of us to tote it," George complained.

"That will attract a lot of attention," Track said.

"We've thought of that, Señor Track," Dr. Cordoba interjected. "We have prepared—how you say—a cover story."

"Of course," Zindel said. "You will pose as a trio of geological prospectors for a large American oil firm. As petroleum men you will have certain tools along. These will be in a special crate. Among the items—unknown to outsiders, of course—will eventually rest Pizarro's calendar, in a special compartment we have prepared."

Cordoba produced a packet of papers from his desk. "These documents will also be in that box. Peru is no different from any other Latin American country. Everyone is impressed by official papers. These should add to your cover."

"If we get policed up and anybody goes under that paperwork, we've had it," Track reminded him.

"It is hoped that no official will inquire further into your activities after looking through these," Cordoba said.

"I hope you're right," Track said. He turned to Zindel. "I presume we'll lug this crate out of the jungle, put in on the next boat back and catch a return train to Lima from this—this town—"

"Iquitos," Zindel volunteered. "Yes, indeed, Mr. Track."

Track was silent for a full minute. "You mentioned we are to get as much information as possible about our contact's sources. Just how much risk is involved in that?"

"I assure you, Mr. Track," Zindel said, "that everything has been as well planned as possible to reduce the danger to yourself and your companions."

Track's patience snapped. "I say again, goddammit, what's the fucking rub? You're making this thing sound a bit too pat to suit me."

"I admit we don't know exactly who you'll be dealing with, Mr. Track," Zindel said. "But since you're a specialist in this sort of thing, we thought using you would guarantee a successful conclusion to the deal."

"Makes sense," Track admitted.

Zindel nodded. "I understand you are on a retainer from The Consortium."

"Yes," Track said. "We went off on our own once and they got pretty upset about it. So they bought our souls."

"Pretty good money though," George said.

"We are legally obligated," Zulu reminded everyone, "and with the type of yearly stipend we are drawing, I am not surprised that The Consortium will use us for undertakings that have even a slight potential of danger or risk. Such situations are our specialty."

"Okay," Track said. "Everybody's made their goddamned point." He looked at Zindel. "We might as well get started as soon as possible. Is our stuff handy?"

"You are to board the morning train," Zindel said. "I must ask you to get to the station early. The train will leave as soon as it is filled with passengers."

Dr. Cordoba was apologetic. "It is a custom of the railroad that serves the rural districts. It might leave as early as 6:00 A.M. or as late as two or three o'clock in the afternoon."

Track's irritation increased. "I'm glad they narrowed it down."

"I'm sorry, Mr. Track," Zindel said. "That's the best we can do."

"What about flying to Iquitos?" George asked.

"The contact wants you on the train," Zindel said. "Perhaps that's where he plans to get in touch with you."

Track looked at his watch. "I presume we have hotel rooms booked."

"Of course," Zindel said. "I shall see personally that you're taken there."

"Fine. We'll meet you outside," Track said. He picked up his bag and motioned to his two friends. "Let's go, guys."

Zulu and George followed him out of the trashy office. They retraced their route down the hall and back outside. As they descended the worn steps to the sidewalk, Track slowly shook his head in uncertainty.

"I have a feeling all this pleasant routine is going to blow up right in our faces."

George Beegh grinned. "Don't it always?"

They waited a few minutes before a limousine pulled up to the curb. Horace Zindel stepped from the back door and held it open for them. "Please step inside, gentlemen," he said good-naturedly. "Your chariot awaits."

A swarthy man, who had been in the front seat beside the driver, quickly took care of their bags.

Track gave the automobile a quick but professional inspection. "Bulletproofed, huh?"

Zindel nodded. "Yes. As an executive of a rather lucrative foreign company, I am a potential target for leftist kidnappers. There is even steel reinforcement in the floorboards."

"That adds quite a bit to the weight, doesn't it?" Track asked.

"I'm afraid so," Zindel answered. "And it plays havoc with our gas mileage."

"It seems a limousine would make a rather conspicuous target anyway," Track said. "Why not use something less flashy?"

"The urban guerrillas would find you out eventually," Zindel said. "So you might as well be prepared from the outset."

As the three got in they noticed that both the driver and the other man in the passenger seat seemed to be real hard-asses. Unsmiling, the two kept a sharp eye on the local area as the car stood by the curb.

Zindel climbed in and joined the others. He turned and nodded to the driver. *"Vámanos."*

"Por su puesto, Señor Zindel," the man responded in a husky voice. The big car pulled away from the curb and eased into the flow of traffic on the avenue.

Across the street, standing in a narrow opening that led to an alley, a small man watched the car. A companion stepped from the shadows into the sunlight. "Was that them?"

The little man, both hands crammed into his suit jacket pockets, answered, "Yes. Did you get a good look at them?"

"Enough to know them like my own family," the larger one said.

"Burn their images into your memory," the little man urged him. "You will meet with them again on the boat out of Iquitos."

"You've already explained that to me," the other said. "I wish to know what else will be happening."

The little man nodded. "*Bueno.* You will be working with three more men."

"¿Pistoleros?"

"Of course! Where do you think we are going? To a choir practice at the cathedral?"

The bigger guy laughed. "With you I'd sooner expect to visit the corridors of hell."

"Never mind the comments," the little man said, "just make sure that you are in Iquitos with three *pistoleros* within a week."

"Who are these *tipos* I am to work with?" the man asked. "Do I know them?"

"You probably do," the small fellow replied. "Right now they are in a position to make sure our friends in the limousine have no trouble when they reach their hotel. I'm afraid that expensive car may tempt certain unruly elements of the city to violent acts against the occupants."

"Good idea," the other said. "Those crazy political types are getting in the way of us honest criminals."

"Most assuredly. Now I am going to join the others who are watching the hotel. Don't forget the rendezvous you are to make, eh?"

"No hay problema," the bigger man commented.

"For your sake there had better be no problem," the smaller man said. "Or the caimans in the Amazon will have more than just the three big hunks of meat I plan to feed them."

The other shuddered involuntarily. "*¡Dios mio!* How I hate reptiles."

The little man smiled without humor. "Keep that in mind." Then, with a slight nod of his head, he left his companion and walked slowly up the street toward a taxi stand.

3

Felipe Rodriguez ran wildly through the clinging jungle vegetation, his fear dulling the pain of the thorns and brambles that tore at the exposed portions of his skin and ripped the ragged clothing he wore.

Behind him, breathing heavily and having difficulty in keeping up, his cousin, Flaco, scrambled in the questionably merciful path that Felipe left in his wake. Finally, drawing a large breath of hot jungle air, Flaco forced himself into a sprint to catch up with the fleeter Felipe and grab his shirt.

"¡Dejame!" Felipe snarled. "Turn me loose!" He slowed enough to turn and belt his cousin across the face.

Flaco yelled in fright and pain, but managed to hold on with the desperate strength of a man maddened with fear. "Don't leave me, Felipe!" he wheezed. "For the love of God!"

"I told you to let go!" Felipe said. He was as frightened as Flaco, but he had the advantage of being strong and healthy. Flaco was a couple of years older but was much weaker, having suffered with TB most of his life.

Felipe hit him again several times.

Flaco was knocked loose, and fell to the jungle floor, rolling in the layers of decayed vegetation that gave off the stench of the grave. He got to his knees and held his hands out in a beseeching gesture to Felipe, who had disappeared into the heavy foliage ahead. "Our mothers were sisters!" Flaco screamed. "What will they say when they find you have abandoned me to the soldiers?"

There was a sudden silence.

Flaco, still on his knees, hung his head and wept in sorrow and despair. He should never have embarked on an outlaw's life with his stronger cousin. It would have been better if he had contented himself with working as a clerk in the small store owned by the mayor of their home village of San Pasqual. But the local girls had openly admired Felipe and the stronger young men. In an area of crushing rural poverty, the profession of banditry was considered as honorable as it was adventurous.

The brave guys swaggered around San Pasqual with their rifles and pistols between forays into neighboring provinces to plunder. They were treated with respect and admiration—particularly by the girls—and the village legends abounded with tales of derring-do that the local boys of the past had performed during various raids for loot.

But Flaco was too weak to be a brave *bandido*. He endured heavy coughing spells while working behind the store counter and running errands or tending to the mayor's burros. In fact, his real name was not Flaco—which meant "skinny"—but Tomas, though no one had ever called him that much. And, to make matters worse, the girls hardly gave him a passing look. When any of the village men came home from successful raids bearing the money and goods they'd taken, the lucky fellows were feted and congratulated. They also enjoyed another bonus. More than one of the local lasses was happily willing to meet with them at some secret place out in the rain forest for a few hours of dallying and lovemaking.

The only time poor Flaco had a chance to take a woman was during infrequent trips with his boss to the town of Rio

Vista on the Amazon River. There, the village boy would pay a few *soles* to some slattern for a quick coupling in a river shack built up on stilts.

Flaco coughed and wiped his hand across his mouth. He looked at the bloody spittle in his palm. He was twenty-three and knew he would never see thirty. Another, more disturbing thought leaped into his mind. If the soldiers caught him, he would never even see that day's sunset. He struggled to his feet in time to see Felipe step back through the thick vegetation and hurry toward him. His stronger cousin was wary, keeping his old Colt .45 pistol ready for any unexpected appearance of soldiers. As an added precaution, he even had some extra shells in his pocket.

Flaco smiled. "You couldn't leave me, eh?"

"Come on, Flaco," Felipe said. "Blood is thicker than water." He bent down and helped his kinsman to his feet. "I don't know why I let you talk me into allowing you to tag along."

"I'm sorry," Flaco said, sincerely apologetic. "But I had to go on a raid—even if only once."

Felipe smiled and winked. "*Seguro*, cousin! You may have a weak body, but you got a strong heart, eh?"

Flaco smiled. "A lot of heart, but no brains."

Felipe laughed. "Let's go. We got to get back to San Pasqual."

"I'm sorry to slow you down."

"Maybe it's better this way," Felipe said. He stuck the pistol in his trouser waistband. "We can be much quieter. If the soldiers can't hear us in the jungle, then they can't find us."

"Then let's go," Flaco said. "If I ever get back to that store in San Pasqual, I will never leave it again."

"Look on the bright side," Felipe said. "You may become a rich man from learning to sell and trade the things we *bandidos* bring home."

"I hope you are right," Flaco said as the two moved deeper into the jungle's tangled growth.

A few hours earlier, the cousins had been moving in the opposite direction with a half dozen other San Paqual men. Their destination had been the town of Rio Vista, where the riverboats had a landing. It was a small commercial center of modest means, but sometimes there were things to tempt *bandidos*. A rumor had come to San Pasqual that a large cache of caiman hides were being stored in Rio Vista prior to shipment down the Amazon to Iquito.

But the rumor of the hides had not only been untrue, it had been manufactured as a trap to lure bandits into the village. A large unit of Peruvian commandos had been concealed in various houses to await the arrival of the raiders.

The San Pasqual men's initial assault on the place had been broken up quickly and efficiently in the hail of machine gun bullets. Pistols and bolt-action rifles stood little chance against such tremendous firepower. The soldiers guaranteed their victory with a prearranged barrage from 60-millimeter mortars that cut off any escape.

It had been by a miracle that Felipe and Flaco had managed to elude bullets and shells and break back into the jungle. But the Peruvian commandos were relentless, proud troops who would have been punished severely by their hard-driving commander if even a sand flea had escaped their deadly fire.

The two escapees, now struggling arm-in-arm through the jungle, had been stubbornly trailed by a well-trained commando squad that was closing in with each passing hour.

THE LIMOUSINE PULLED to the curb in front of a modest but clean hotel located in the southern outskirts of Lima. Dan Track glanced out the window of the car at the narrow three-story building sandwiched between a restaurant and a drugstore. He looked at Horace Zindel. "Not real fancy."

"Sorry," Zindel said. "But it was thought best you put up here rather than in a fancier place downtown. You're not apt to attract so much attention here."

Zulu wasn't as disappointed as Track. "It appears to be a rather pleasant hostelry," he remarked.

"Indeed it is," Zindel said. "The restaurant next door is in the same category. The menu is not haute cuisine, but the food is quite delicious nevertheless."

George Beegh shrugged. "Everything looks fine with me." He reached for the door handle.

"Please wait," Zindel said with a smile. He leaned forward and knocked on the window that separated them from the chauffeur and his companion. *"Estamos listos para salir."*

The man riding shotgun nodded. *"Bien."*

Zindel looked at his guests. "It is customary for the driver and his partner to check out the street before one steps from one's automobile."

Track was impatient. "Fuck it." He hit the door and quickly stepped out onto the sidewalk.

The fusillade from the adjoining alley swept the bodyguard off his feet and threw him, bloody and quite dead, back so hard into Track that the American fell to the gutter. But Track had instinctively whipped the Beretta auto from his shoulder holster.

Zulu and George, having reacted in their usual fashion, were outside on the opposite side of the limo with the driver. Horace Zindel, crouched on the floor in the back, shrieked at them. "Get back inside! Hurry! The bodyguards will handle the situation!"

But the continuing salvo of shots finally took out the chauffeur. The man, hit several times in the torso, staggered out into the middle of the street. He fired a wild shot that ricocheted off the hotel before a headshot exploded his skull and dumped him unceremoniously to the pavement.

Track and Company had instantly pinpointed the location of the attacker. All three of their pistols barked, sending slugs flying across the patrons of the café who had gone to cover under their tables.

A gunman unwisely exposed himself to the trio in a valiant but stupid attempt to get in some telling shots. He got them—three simultaneous hits in the chest that flung him back against the wall of the building behind him. He managed to lurch forward and aim again, but his face disintegrated under a single shot from Track's automatic.

Two more men leaped from cover and cut loose with a fusillade, forcing Track, Zulu and George to get behind the limousine.

"I'm going around the block and coming up behind those bastards," Track said. "Throw enough firepower out there to make them duck, then I'll make my move."

"Righto, Dan," Zulu said.

Fresh volleys from another direction rocked the big automobile and sparks flew from the body. Track and his two friends emptied what was left of their magazines and inserted loaded ones as they turned toward this fresh assault.

"Jesus!" Track hissed. "This might be a spontaneous ambush, but they've worked up a cross-fire pattern on us."

Zulu methodically returned fire. "Well-trained chaps, what?"

"Damn!" Track said irritably. "Should we go over there and congratulate the bastards?" He cut loose with four rapid-fire shots.

"It's only that I admire real professionalism," Zulu said.

The first two bushwhackers now renewed their efforts. George glanced around. "We're between the rock and that hard place. We can't stay and we can't leave."

Track grimly returned fire. Within a few minutes he and his two comrades in arms would be out of ammunition. If help or relief didn't arrive, the ambushers would be able to knock them off at will.

FLACO WHEEZED PAINFULLY, his face pale as his eyes rolled upward. Unable to speak, he sucked in the hot air as his ravaged lungs tried to consume as much oxygen as possible.

Felipe, his arm around his cousin's waist, half carrying him, finally stopped. "We shall rest awhile."

Flaco collapsed to the wet ground. He gestured weakly for several moments before he could speak. "Go...go on.... I can't make it...." His voice was weak and he tried to push against Felipe to urge him to go. "I am...not worth...the risk...."

"I'll decide that, cousin," Felipe whispered. "Try not to talk. The soldiers will hear us."

Flaco nodded and closed his eyes. He had never been so exhausted in all his life. His legs felt as if they were made of melted rubber. They offered no support, and would not respond to his efforts to rise. He knew he had to face the truth.

"Please...Felipe...go away...."

It was a grand gesture. A display of supreme courage and unselfishness. Flaco felt it would be the only chance in his entire, miserable existence to show that, despite his physical weaknesses, he was as much a man as anyone.

But Felipe Rodriguez was no less brave. He was ashamed of the cowardly way he had acted before. "I cannot leave you."

"I am not afraid," Flaco said.

Felipe patted him gently on the shoulder. "I know you are not. When we are back in the village I will tell everyone how you urged me to leave you."

Flaco smiled sadly and shook his head. "I will never see San Pasqual again."

"Do not babble like a fool!"

Flaco started to speak again, but his mouth would not work. He could see the soldier's face, the man's features distorted by the streaked camouflage paint, peering through the vegetation a couple of meters away.

The trooper, his MAT-49 submachine gun at the ready, stepped out into view. He had a reason to feel no fear. He was immediately joined by four others.

"¡Las manos arriba!" the soldier commanded.

Felipe instantly obeyed, putting his hands high over his head. But Flaco, in his fatigue, was slow—too slow.

Five short bursts of 9-millimeter slugs ripped into his wasted body, smashing his brittle bones and churning his emaciated flesh into pulverized meat.

TRACK ASSESSED THE SITUATION as best as he could. He was severely limited by time and the circumstances that were rapidly deteriorating.

"Our only chance is to break for the hotel door," he said.

"There ain't any ammo inside there," George protested.

"But there is cover," Zulu interjected. "I agree. The choice of action is extremely narrow."

"What about Zindel in the car?" George asked.

"He can shut the door and hope they don't pack plastic explosive all over that vehicle," Track said.

The incoming fire picked up rapidly until they were surrounded by a man-made steel hailstorm.

"Shit!" Track swore. "We'll be lucky if we make it ourselves."

"Let's quit talking and get moving," George said impatiently.

"Okay," Track agreed. "Get ready—"

More fire suddenly exploded. The trio was forced to duck lower. "What the hell?" Track asked of no one in particular. "Is there a whole goddamn urban guerrilla army after us?"

Zulu observed for a moment. "By Jove! There's some other chaps here all right, but they're not firing at us."

"He's right," George said. "They're after the other guys. Maybe the cops have finally shown up."

The fighting continued for a full five minutes before a sudden silence announced the end of the small battle. Track took advantage of the unexpected ceasefire to leap out from behind the car.

But all combatants involved, other than themselves, had disappeared. He caught sight of a small man in a white tropical suit rushing away down the street.

Within five minutes the street was back to normal except for five dead men scattered around the scene of the recent combat. Track reholstered the Beretta as Horace Zindel joined him.

"What happened?" Zindel asked. "I thought we'd had it."

"Somebody pulled our asses out of some pretty deep shit," Track said. "And I guarantee I'll find out who and why."

Zindel wiped at the perspiration on his face. "It could be, Mr. Track, that seeking that information will get you in even more trouble than you've just escaped."

Track smiled sardonically. "I guess that curious cats and guys like me don't stand much of a chance."

4

The five soldiers were pissed off. The camouflage paint on their faces was sweat streaked and worn away. Large, wet areas of perspiration soaked their uniforms, and even parts of their web gear were damp.

Felipe Rodriguez looked from them down at the bullet-mangled body of his cousin Flaco. He turned his head back in time to receive a heavy punch to the face. The blow sent him staggering backward and he stumbled over the cadaver, falling heavily to the ground.

The soldier who had hit him, a corporal, walked over and pulled the old pistol from Felipe's trouser waistband. He aimed the young bandit's own weapon down at him. "On your feet, *hijo de la chingada*!" the trooper said, cursing Felipe and his mother.

Felipe's jaw ached dully from his chin to the back of his ears. He put his hands down to push himself up. The corporal kicked hard. The jump boot hit the young bandit's chest, and flipped him over on his back.

"Keep your mitts over your head!"

Felipe, obeying, struggled to his feet with difficulty. He finally stood, but swayed a bit as he fought to maintain his balance. The corporal continued to display his irritation by delivering three stinging slaps that whipped Felipe's head back and forth.

"Are you proud of yourself, *puerco*?"

Felipe, who didn't particularly like being called a pig, declined to answer. The reward for his sullen silence was another series of openhanded smacks followed by a straight jab to the face. He went down again.

"On your feet! On your feet!" the corporal screamed.

Felipe started to struggle again—then he stopped. He stared furiously up at the soldier. "If you are going to shoot me, do it! I won't play your stupid games in the meantime."

The corporal grinned wickedly. "Why, amigo! I am not going to shoot you. I am going to give you an invitation to join your other friends to meet my sergeant."

The other troopers laughed loudly. "He will like Zotol, eh?"

"Of course," the corporal said. "And I am sure that Sergeant Zotol is going to be crazy about him, too." He pointed back in the direction of the town of Rio Vista. "Let's go, bandit. The justice of Colonel Torres and Sergeant Zotol awaits your charming presence."

As Felipe got to his feet, he risked one more look at Flaco. His dead cousin lay in the deep jungle shadows, his open eyes staring upward. Felipe swallowed hard.

Poor Flaco, he thought, born to endure the torments of a deadly disease, then not even able to suffer a quiet dignified death at the hands of God.

The corporal allowed Felipe to rest his hands on top of his head as he was shoved through the thick underbrush. Unable to shield his face, all he could do was close his eyes tight as branches and thorns tore at him.

After an hour's fast walking they emerged onto a wide bank along the Amazon. The going was easier now, though striding through the soft, sandy soil was tiring.

Felipe glanced out into the river and could see the bodies of several men drifting slowly with the current.

The corporal laughed. "Those are some of your friends. Rotten *bandidos* don't get Christian burials after the soldiers of Colonel Torres kill them."

The cadavers were bloated beyond recognition. But Felipe did see a red shirt that he thought belonged to a close friend of his. He turned his eyes away and trudged on.

After another thirty minutes, Felipe could see the ramshackle buildings of Rio Vista. The dock where the river steamer tied up extended out over the water. There were a number of soldiers standing there guarding a half dozen prisoners, who were sitting with their hands on top of their heads.

A muscular, short trooper walked from the dock toward them. When he reached them, Felipe was grabbed roughly and shoved down to a squatting position.

The newcomer spoke in a low, husky voice. "Where is the other one, Corporal?"

"He is dead, *mi sargento*," the man reported.

"I wanted them both—*los dos*."

"Yes, Sergeant. But the other was a weak, sickly man who coughed blood. No waste in his death."

The sergeant reached down and grabbed Felipe, hauling him to his feet as easily as if the prisoner was weightless. "Was there something wrong with the other bastard who ran away with you?"

Felipe stared into the most brutal face he'd ever seen in his life. The eyes, with no brows, were mere slits. The man's nose was a formless flat mass set above a cruel gash of a mouth.

Felipe was suddenly punched in the kidneys from behind. The corporal's voice in his ear was angry. "Answer the sergeant!"

Felipe licked his lips. "He was sick with *el consumo*."

The sergeant twisted his mouth into a lopsided grin. "You stinking bandits must have been desperate to bring along a sick man."

The corporal giggled. "And pretty stupid to fall for that story about caiman hides, eh?"

The sergeant, without further comment, nodded toward the dock.

Felipe was prodded forward. He struggled through the mud and climbed up the bank where the earth was firmer. Curious townspeople had gathered to watch. They grinned openly at the prisoner as he was marched onto the dock and made to sit down with the others. A couple of the people leaned toward him and spit. They had no love for the outlaws who raided their village and made jungle travel dangerous and uncertain.

The sergeant joined them, and stared coldly at his prisoners. A couple of the tougher captives engaged in a staring contest with him, but finally averted their eyes from the cruel face that seemed marked by the devil to the superstitious country bandits.

When he finally spoke to them, the words from that brutish mouth were abrupt and cold.

"I am Sergeant Zotol. I am going to take you to hell." Then he turned and walked off the dock.

The other soldiers immediately jumped into action. "Get up! Pronto! Quickly!"

The corporal walked up to Felipe and grinned. "You think you've just met the devil, eh?"

Felipe answered truthfully. "I think so."

But the corporal shook his head. "Oh, no, *bandido*. You've only met his prime minister."

Another soldier laughed. "And he was telling you no lies. Sergeant Zotol is truly taking you to hell!"

DAN TRACK STOOD in the darkness of his hotel room and stared down at the street below. Passersby now strolled nonchalantly through an area that had been the scene of the brief but explosive gun battle only a few hours previously.

Track took a sip from the drink he held. The Seagrams Seven over the rocks was mellow and satisfying. He was sharing his most preferred drink with his least favorite part of the day—early evening.

These were the brief but bitter hours that brought thoughts of Desiree Goth into his psyche with the most persistence. The memories taunted him, reminding him that he had lost her—and still wanted her—with a piercing longing that ripped through him like a spear.

Track finished the drink and walked across the room to the tray that held the ice bucket and liquor bottle. He quickly mixed another and had started back toward the window when a knock interrupted him.

He pulled the Beretta from the shoulder holster and set the drink down at the same time.

Another knock followed—then two more, one, and another two.

Track went to the door and rapped twice, then opened it.

George Beegh and Hodari Zulu stepped inside. The prearranged signal was a bit tedious at times, but it had saved them from nasty situations—both inside *and* outside rooms they were going into or out of.

"Jesus! It's gloomy in here," George complained. "Why don't you turn on some lights?"

"I like to drink in the dark," Track said. "What's up?"

Zulu sat down on the bed. "George and I thought we would explore a bit of Lima's nightlife."

"Yeah," George said enthusiastically. "Particularly since it looks like we'll be out in the Amazonian jungle for a while."

"Hell!" Track scoffed. "We were in Las Vegas not a week ago."

"All the more reason to go," George said. "This way we'll sort of ease back into operations, huh?"

"Care to join us, Dan?" Zulu asked.

"No thanks," Track said. "I think I'll just—" He hesitated. After a quick glance around the lonely room, he reconsidered. "Yeah! Hell, yes! I'd like to get out for a good time."

"Fantastic!" Zulu said. "What do you say we change and meet back here in a half hour?"

"Let's make it twenty minutes," George suggested. "I hate to think of depriving any Hispanic beauties of my company for any more time than is absolutely necessary."

Track suddenly felt good. He slapped George on the shoulder. "Your modesty is only exceeded by your vulgar personality."

"I know," George said, grinning, "ain't I awful?"

"Twenty minutes then," Zulu said. "Let's get cracking."

THE NIGHT INSECTS BUZZED and chirped through the thick, hot jungle air. Felipe Rodriguez and the other prisoners, manacled together, lay in the clearing trying to sleep. Despite their exhaustion, fear kept all of them in a state of wakefulness. Each tread of the sentry's boots made their eyes pop open in grim anticipation.

Even if Sergeant Zotol hadn't already taken them to hell, he'd gotten them close enough that day to feel the heat and smell the brimstone.

They had spent the majority of the day being kicked and pummeled into keeping up with the rapidly striding sergeant. Although all the bandits had been born and reared in the area, the exertion required to keep pace in the steamy weather had taken a terrific toll on their stamina and conditioning. Numerous blows from submachine gun stocks had not helped a lot either.

Many had been reduced to near nakedness when their clothing was ripped and shredded by the sharp branches and thorns of bushes. Insects and leeches had grabbed on to the exposed flesh in an orgy of biting, stinging and bloodsucking. These bites were now ugly swollen sores, oozing fluids that attracted even more of the parasites and pests.

Felipe, lying in the thick, itchy grass, rolled over slowly to avoid jostling the two men on either side of him. He managed to get fairly comfortable, despite having his hands cuffed behind him, and fell into fitful sleep filled with bad dreams.

TRACK, USED TO BEING IN THE OPEN AIR, found the thick, smoky atmosphere of the club stifling. But Zulu and George—particularly George—were having one hell of a good time.

Drinking and laughing, they danced with available women at every opportunity, and George narrowly avoided getting into a couple of fights with jealous escorts.

Track drank slowly and quietly. He wasn't particularly enjoying himself, but he had to admit it was better than sitting in that damned hotel room alone.

The orchestra, a typical Latin-American type with a plethora of rhythm instruments, brought the song it was playing to a halt. The dancers reluctantly left the floor and returned to their tables. George and Zulu sat down after signaling to the waiter that they wanted refills.

"The broad's crazy about me," George said confidently of the girl he'd just danced with.

Zulu laughed in his deep, pleasurable way. "Is there romance in the air for you then, young George?"

"Sure. If I could get her to leave that dickhead she's with," George said. He winked at a young woman sitting across the room. Her boyfriend glowered in sullen anger.

"You'd better cool it," Track said. "Those hispanic guys don't like anybody flirting with their women."

George laughed. "Look who's talking. What about the singer, huh?"

"What about her?" Track asked, thinking of the beautiful songstress who came out now and then to sing with the orchestra.

"She's eyeing you, Dan," Zulu said. "I swear she is singing directly to you as if there was no one else in the room."

Track scoffed. "Bullshit!"

"Our boy is not exaggerating a bit," Zulu said.

Track felt a sudden surge of pleasure. He had admitted to himself that Desiree's departure had not only hurt him but had bruised his masculine ego a bit. Maybe what he needed was for some woman to fall for him hard. That would be better than the sincere compliments of a professional whore.

George started to make a remark, but the master of ceremonies, a smooth-looking Peruvian, stepped in front of the band. "*Señores y señoras, me da mucho gusto de presentar la bellissima cantora*—Ana Garanta." Then, for the benefit of the tourists present, he introduced the singer again, in English.

The woman stepped into the soft spotlight holding a microphone in her hand. She was most certainly beautiful, a dazzler with soft Hispanic features; her hair was a deep brunette and her eyes black and flashing. All this contrasted nicely with alabaster skin—particularly where her breasts swelled above the plunging neckline of her gown.

Ana's voice was velvety and she sang the song in her native Spanish, each note seeming to be an involuntary expression of her passion and desire. She moved slowly around the room until she reached the table where Track and his friends sat. Then she sang to Track, lulling him with dark eyes full of promise, her mouth suggestively wooing the microphone.

She ended the song amid enthusiastic applause and shouts. After giving Track one more bold look, she went back to the band and left the microphone on the piano before going offstage.

George leaned toward his uncle. There was excitement in his voice. "She's wild about you, man! Write her a note."

Zulu laid a huge hand on Track's shoulder. "The song she was singing to you is called 'Besame Mucho'—it means 'Kiss Me a Lot.' And I agree with George. Do, most assuredly, send her a note, Dan!"

"Okay, okay," Track said. "I'll invite her to the table." He scribbled on a napkin and called the waiter over. "Take this to the singer, please."

The waiter nodded. *"Sí, señor."* He returned empty-handed a couple of minutes later.

Track looked at him. "She couldn't make it, right?"

"Al contrario, señor," the waiter said. "Señorita Garanta extends an invitation for you to visit her in her dressing room."

George shook his head in open admiration. "Damn, Uncle Dan, you are truly my hero!"

Zulu laughed. "And mine too!"

Track stood up and grinned. "Tell Mom I stayed late at the library."

George laughed. "I presume we shouldn't wait up for you."

"Correct," Track said. He turned to the waiter. "Lead the way, my good man."

5

Ana Garanta's dressing room door was opened by a young Indian woman wearing a colorful, handwoven dress of the type native to Peru. She curtsied politely and stood aside to allow Track to enter.

Track, thinking she was cute, smiled at her. "Thank you."

"La señorita estará con usted muy pronto."

"Pardon me?" Track said.

The girl, a teenager, gestured toward a sofa. *"Siéntase, señor."*

Track guessed she meant for him to sit down. He looked at the girl and smiled again.

The little Indian giggled. *"Con permiso, señor."* Then she scurried through another door.

Track glanced around the sitting room. The singer obviously did not change clothes in there. The small chamber was set up for entertaining and relaxing. A miniature wet bar stood in one corner. Besides the sofa that Track occupied, there were two comfortable chairs. A mahogany coffee table, with cigarette case and ashtray on it, sat solidly on the floor in front of him. A couple of avant-garde watercolor paintings hung on the wall.

After only a five-minute wait, the door to the other room opened and the woman entered. Track noted that she was even more beautiful in normal room light. He stood up as she walked across to him with an outstretched hand.

"My name is Dan Track," he said, noting both the grace with which she moved and evidence provided by the light behind her that she wore nothing beneath the colorful kimono that adorned her lithe body.

"I am Ana Garanta," she said. "Please to call me Ana."

"And please call me Dan," Track said. "You speak excellent English."

She seemed genuinely pleased. "Oh, thank you. I was almost two years in Hollywood. Between bit parts I study the English. But I never was a star."

"The public's loss," Track said gallantly.

"You are too kind," Ana said. She gestured at the sofa. "Please to sit down, Dan."

"Thanks." He felt he should say something about her professional abilities. "It seems you speak quite well in English and sing very beautifully in Spanish."

"You are most nice to say it." She joined Track, sitting close to him. "It was good of you to invite me to a drink. So, now I invite you to one."

Track liked her slight twist of English. "And I happily accept."

Ana turned toward the door. "Lupita! Lupita!" She looked back at Track. "What is your pleasure?"

"You mean for a drink?"

Ana laughed lightly. "Of course. I have everything behind that small bar, believe me."

"I do," Track said, then to himself, and you got plenty beneath that kimono, too!

The Indian girl came in and curtsied to them. *"¿Sí, señorita?"*

"Quiero un vino blanco, y el señor—" She nodded to Track. "What do you wish?"

Track didn't want to sink into any alcoholic hazes. He ruled out hard liquor. "A beer would be fine, thanks."

"Una cerveza para el señor."

Lupita curtsied and happily scurried to the bar. Within a few seconds she was back, carrying a tray with a glass of white wine and an open bottle of Peruvian beer complete with a frosted mug.

Ana smiled at the young girl. *"Gracias, Lupita. Dejanos ahora por favor."*

There was another curtsy, followed by a shy glance at Track, then the Indian girl left them.

"I dismissed her," Ana explained. "She's a lovely child, a treasure. But there are times when—how you say—three peoples is a crowd, no?"

"Yes," Track said, agreeing emphatically. He poured the beer into the mug and raised it in a toast. "To us."

Ana lifted her own glass. "To us." She took a dainty sip. "What are you doing in Peru, Dan?"

Such questions always made Track suspicious, no matter how innocently they might be asked. He went straight into the cover story of being part of a geological survey team assigned to inspect oil prospects in the Amazon basin just east of the Andes. This led to twenty minutes of small talk on topics ranging from American/Peruvian life-styles, movies and music. The conversation finally gravitated to the fact that neither of them was married. It might have gone on for another half hour but Track suddenly set the beer mug on the table. He gently took her glass and did the same with it.

Then he leaned forward and kissed Ana Garanta lightly on the mouth.

The woman responded immediately, pressing heavily against him, her arms quickly entwining his neck. Track's hand went around her waist as he returned her passion, then he slowly slid it up to her breast, softly kneading the fleshy mound and then slipping inside the kimono.

"Ah!" she gasped in pleasure as she broke off the kiss. Ana looked into Track's eyes, her expression reminding him of what a tigress in heat must look like. Her voice was low and sultry. "I wanted you the first moment I look upon you out there."

Track knew that if she wasn't a nympho, she sure as hell was the closest thing he'd ever find to one. "Is that why you sang to me?"

"Yes, Dan!" She kissed him again as he untied the sash holding the kimono closed. Her breasts, large but taut, were exposed and she thrust them toward him in an unconscious display of animal lust and yearning.

They did it the first time on the sofa. Track didn't recall stripping, but strip he did, carefully keeping his Beretta handy. If Ana noticed the pistol, she gave no indication of it.

Track mounted her as she flung one foot over the back of the couch. This was a woman who wanted sex and said so in an unabashed, uncontrolled drive that she neither worried about nor was able to control. Ana Garanta gasped and heaved against him, her long fingernails raking his bare back as they rocked rhythmically.

She climaxed first, her pulsations finally bringing Track to his peak. By then they were streaked with each other's perspiration, and the light from the room's only lamp glistened off their bodies.

Track, his face nestled against her neck, smiled secretly. Hot damn! he said to himself, I really needed that!

Slowly, reluctantly, they disengaged. Track knew it would be strictly up to her if it would be an all-night affair. Her next words confirmed it would be a few hours before he'd leave. "I have a big bathtub in the next room. Shall we use it?"

"Let's," Track said, always the gracious guest. As he picked up his clothes, he made sure the automatic was not out of reach.

Ana, a woman born and raised in a machismo Latin American world, didn't think it unusual for a man to tote a piece. Thus, she made no remarks about it. She simply took his hand and led him through the door into the next room.

The warm water and scented soap set them both off again. This time they did it standing up, with Ana braced on the side of the tub. The small room echoed her loud rasping breath that built to a cry.

The third time was on the bed. The two followed this up with some refreshments from the bar and more talking until their ardor returned.

Track spent another three hours with Ana Garanta. The last half of the visit was in a street café where they refreshed their drained energy with hot, thick coffee and *panes dulces* covered with plenty of powdered sugar and real butter.

It was midmorning when Track returned to the hotel. He stepped from the cab after a quick but careful scrutiny of the street, and paid the driver. He glanced around once more as he reached the front door—and stopped.

He recognized the short man in the soiled white suit standing in the shadows across the street as the one who had appeared after the gunfight. Track did not let on that he had noticed him and went into the lobby. He quickly turned and raced to the heavily curtained window. He looked out and saw the man just as he stepped back into the alley and disappeared.

Track let the curtain fall back into place, then walked rapidly to the elevator.

THE COLUMN OF EXHAUSTED PRISONERS staggered out of the jungle. Some fell or pulled against their chains, causing the men to whom they were manacled to be painfully jerked and yanked.

Felipe Rodriguez looked up to see that they were approaching a large stockade. The rain forest had been cleared away fifty meters from the walls. There were guard towers at each corner, and a long entanglement of barbed wire was twisted on frames built onto the top of the log wall.

He could see a sign nailed above the huge double-portaled entrance to the interior of the prison. As they neared it, he made out the words: SE GANA LIBERTAD POR TRABAJO.

He spoke them softly to himself, "Freedom is won through work." He felt a glimmer of hope. Perhaps, after a time, if he did as he was told, the soldiers might let him go.

"Halt!" Sergeant Zotol's voice boomed over the scene. He barked a few terse orders, and his troopers suddenly went into a frenzy of punching, kicking and pushing the prisoners into a more orderly line. When that was accomplished, the two doors to the stockade were opened, and the group of miserable bandits was rudely ushered inside.

More of the pummeling continued after the portals were closed. When the soldiers were finally satisfied with the formation, they stepped back with submachine guns ready.

Felipe closed his eyes, thinking they were to be executed, but the only sound was a barked command from Sergeant Zotol:

"¡Silencio!"

Felipe was startled alert and glanced around the area. The stockade grounds were large—two hundred and fifty meters on each side. He discovered there were only three walls. Where the fourth one would have been a mountain acted as a natural barrier. Felipe could see a cavelike entrance that was reinforced with timbers. Beside it, running down to a creek that wound its way across the middle of the compound, was a sluice arrangement of some sort.

There were men working around the contraption. After a few moments, a trio of men appeared from the entrance, each pushing a small wheelbarrow. They halted at the sluice and emptied the contents of the wheelbarrows—which appeared to be no more than dirt—into it. Then, while other men pushed this down the troughlike device, the three wheeled the barrows back to the interior of the "cave."

Curiosity momentarily erased Felipe's fear, but Zotol's voice sounded once again, loud and clear: "Prisoners! Attention!"

The soldiers stood ramrod straight as another of their kind strode out in front of the captives. This newcomer also wore a uniform of a camouflage pattern, but his was carefully tailored and there were colorful pins on the shoulders. He carried a short riding crop in his hands. But what made Felipe hold the man in awe was the fact that Sergeant Zotol treated him with great respect and deference.

The man turned to the prisoners, then walked up close to them. He was smiling. "*Buenos días, muchachos*. Welcome to Camp Oro. I am Colonel Torres, the commandant."

Torres was a bit plumpish in the face, but his body was slim and taut. The prisoners felt as if they were being addressed by a wealthy landowner.

"You have been brought here because you have violated the laws of the republic," Torres continued. "But the government, your benefactor, is not vengeful or angry with you. Only disappointed. *El presidente* and all his cabinet officers want you to be good citizens. So they have turned you over to me for a fresh education that will give you a new outlook on life."

Felipe was surprised that the government—that faraway entity that lived in Lima—would have any knowledge of or interest in an aborted bandit raid on a miserable river town like Rio Vista.

"This schooling I shall give you," Torres said, "will not be done with books. It will be done with hard, honest labor as you pay back the government for the benevolent and merciful love it shows for you." He pointed to what Felipe thought was a cave. "There is a gold mine there, prisoners. You will work hard to remove that precious metal so that the Peruvian people will be able to purchase the materials and knowledge necessary to make them a world power." Torres smiled. "Did you all see the sign over the gate when you came in here?"

No one said anything. They simply stared at the army officer in silence. Zotol walked behind the ranks of the prisoners and shoved one forward. It was Felipe.

Torres approached Felipe with a kindly expression on his face. He pointed the riding crop at him. "Did you see the sign, *muchacho*?"

Felipe fearfully nodded his head.

Torres continued to smile. "What did it say?"

Felipe cleared his throat. "I think it said 'Freedom is won through work,' Excellency."

Torres's smile widened. "*¡Muy bien!* A smart lad like you should do well here in Camp Oro, no?" He looked at the others. "The sign spoke the truth. Freedom is most assuredly won here by work. Work hard, *muchachos*, and you'll soon be trusted citizens of Peru again. You will be allowed to return to your homes and families as better men. And you'll have a bit of money in your pockets, too."

Felipe felt better then. He was willing to work, and work hard if that was necessasry. He spoke out. "How long must we labor here before we can leave, Excellency?"

Zotol, standing beside him, instantly whirled to face Felipe. He hit the youth hard in the mouth with a large fist. The young bandit collapsed to the hard-packed dirt. The sergeant used hard, vicious kicks to get him back to his feet.

Torres's voice was calm. "But we have rules here, *muchachos*. Never speak to me or any soldier unless you have permission. There are other regulations here, but you'll learn them soon enough." He waved his riding crop, then turned and strolled away.

Felipe dabbed at the blood on his mouth. Whatever feelings of relief and optimisim he'd had before melted away. The corporal and the other soldiers had not lied to him back in Rio Vista.

He truly was in hell.

6

The day had been a long and miserable one for Felipe Rodriguez and his fellow prisoners.

They had done none of the work that Colonel Torres promised would bring them freedom. Instead they spent the entire day going through a special softening-up process under the supervision of Sergeant Zotol. The main purpose of the activity was to introduce them to discipline and break whatever streaks of rebellion and insubordination might be left over after the long walk through the jungle.

The first thing on their agenda was haircuts. Each newcomer soon looked like the old-timers after their heads had been clipped close with military barber clippers.

After that, the principal lesson began when Sergeant Zotol—with several submachine gun-toting soldiers accompanying him—faced the assembled prisoners. The sergeant held up a square piece of cardboard that had been painted solid black. He asked a simple question of his audience. "What color is this?"

None of the prisoners answered.

Zotol reacted to their silence by charging into their small group and indiscriminately kicking and punching a few of them around. He glared at his victims as they hurriedly got back to their feet. Then he went back to the front of the class. "What color is this?"

"Black," came the response.

Zotol pointed to one of the captives. "Step up here with me."

The man reluctantly joined the sergeant.

Zotol held up the cardboard. "What color is this?"

"*Es negro*—it is black."

The sergeant kicked the man in the groin. "What color is this?"

The prisoner, on the ground doubled up, again answered, "Black."

There was another kick. "Incorrect. *Es blanco.* It is white."

The injured man stared at the black cardboard and nodded. "Yes—yes, it is white."

Zotol pointed at another man. "What color is this?"

"White."

To yet another. "You!"

"White."

"And you!"

"White."

"Yes. It is white because I say it is white," Zotol said. "That is your first—and most important—lesson. Whatever we say here is correct and proper. You must never argue or disagree at any time."

The prisoners, simple men without schooling, would never philosophize about the experience. To them it was an uncomplicated matter: a man, stronger, better armed and with others of his ilk close by, could push them around. The abstract idea that he operated on authority granted him by a faraway government meant nothing to the outlaws.

"And now," Zotol said, "you will learn another important lesson about the cardinal sins of Camp Oro. This one will pertain to punishments given out for disobedience and disrespect."

The line of convicts was led across the large yard to a place where a grouping of small oblong huts was situated. The structures were made of planks that had been caulked airtight. The only openings in them were narrow slits in the doors. A nearby guard took his cue from the sergeant and pulled a ring of keys from his cartridge belt. He went over to one of the structures and unlocked the door. Reaching inside, he pulled a naked prisoner out.

The unfortunate man blinked hard against the sunlight. His dry, flaky skin showed the terrible ravages of dehydration. Unable to stand, he sank to his knees, but at least had the strength to raise his hands in a beseeching gesture. "*Agua*," he begged. "Water."

Zotol looked at the guard. "When was the last time this worm was given a drink?"

"Yesterday, Sergeant."

Zotol laughed. "Well, we don't want to spoil him, do we? He gets his next refreshment tomorrow. Return him to his suite."

The guard grabbed the man and flung him back into the shack that was little more than a box.

"He talked back to a guard," Zotol explained. "For that he will spend seven days and nights in his coffin." He pointed upward to the blazing sun. "It is hot out here, no? In that little 'hotel' of his, the temperature can go up another twenty-five or even fifty degrees during the midday."

The lesson was well taken by the group.

"There is one more thing for you to see," Zotol said. "We have a criminal who committed the worst crime possible here at Camp Oro, a crime even worse than striking a guard—he tried to run away."

The sergeant marched the captives around the little houses to an open area behind them. This was a spot where the sun pounded from dawn to dusk like a white-hot hammer on a baking anvil.

A man, burned black by the relentless rays, lay spread-eagled, tied to four stakes driven into the ground. Lying faceup, he absorbed the full fury of the burning disk in the sky.

"This piece of shit thought he could escape us," Zotol explained calmly as if he were describing a sleeping dog. "He not only learned he could not, but he also was made aware of the wrathful vengeance of myself and *el coronel* Torres. I want you each to walk by slowly, and gaze carefully at this stupid carrion. And, *por Dios en el cielo*, take heed, you scum!"

Felipe shuffled forward in his place in line. When he drew abreast of the man on the ground he looked at him. He noted the man was not a Hispanic. He was a European and, despite the wretched condition of his skin, it was obvious he was a white man. His features were not like those of an Indian or mestizo, yet there was something even stranger about the face. Felipe unconsciously looked closer to determine what was so strange about the unfortunate convict.

Then, in horror, he saw.

They had cut away his eyelids. The poor wretch's eyesight had been seared away by the sun as he'd stared unblinkingly up into the blazing orb.

Zotol reformed his unhappy little group. "You are now going to spend the rest of the day learning one of the fine skills of soldiering. We are going to teach you to march, which means before this evening, you will be able to move about smartly and efficiently in a group." He laughed. "Of course some of you will learn slower than others. But, please, don't worry about it. My drill instructors carry nice mahogany batons to punctuate the lessons. Even the most stupid mule among you will look quite soldierly in a remarkably short time."

Felipe Rodriguez, his mind still swimming with pictures of the poor sufferer behind the huts, swallowed hard. He offered up a silent and quick, but sincere prayer for guidance and aid in the ordeal he knew he was to face.

"The first lesson," Zotol announced, "will be how to properly assume the position of attention. Shall we begin? *¡Bueno!* Squad—*a-ten-cion*!"

The corporal and two picked men carrying batons moved in to assist in the instruction.

TRACK, ZULU AND GEORGE SAT at one of the rear tables in the outdoor restaurant located next to their hotel. They had chosen the site, not to avoid the sidewalk foot traffic, but because it prevented anyone from approaching them without first being spotted. The trio faced outward, the Berettas loosened in the shoulder holsters they wore under their loose jackets.

George sipped his coffee. "You haven't said much about last night, Dan."

Track shrugged. "What's to say? I got laid."

"About time," George remarked. He knew nothing of Track's episode with the Las Vegas call girls. "Are you going to see her again?"

"Maybe after we get back," Track said. "She's going up north to visit her family, then off to see an old friend for a couple of weeks or so."

Zulu nodded knowingly. "It would seem she is keeping you well informed of her future plans, Dan, old boy. I should think it a logical conclusion that she is doing so in order to facilitate your arranging to see her again."

"Yeah, she is," Track said. He smiled despite himself. "That woman is what I call a rip-roaring piece of ass. She wanted to get laid, relaid and par-laid—and she made no silly pretenses about it."

"A regular nympho, huh?" George asked eagerly. "She got a sister? Or a cousin, maybe?" He laughed out loud. "Hell, what about her ol' granny, for chrissake!"

"You're not that horny, are you?"

"I'm always that horny," George said.

The trio quieted down as the waiter approached their table and served their meal. They'd each ordered a thick steak, salad and fried potatoes.

Track cut into his medium-well-done slab of beef. "I meant to ask you two something," he said just before slipping a hunk of the excellent meat into his mouth. He chewed a few times. "Have you noticed a little guy wearing a dirty white suit hanging around?"

George shook his head. "Not me."

"Nor I," Zulu answered. "But obviously you have."

"Yeah," Track said thoughtfully. "He was there on the day of the firefight in front of the hotel. I saw him again this morning when I got back from Ana's place."

"Perhaps it was just a coincidence," Zulu suggested. "He might live or work here in the neighborhood."

"I don't think so," Track said, spearing some salad with his fork. "He was staked out for some reason or another."

George shrugged. "Don't worry about it. We're leaving in the morning anyway."

"I'll be glad about that," Track admitted. He hunched his shoulders in an unconscious movement. "There's something strange—even evil—about this mission we're on."

"Hell!" George exclaimed. "We aren't really on it yet."

"Yeah," Track agreed. "And that's really got me worried!"

"And now, so am I," Zulu said. "Your intuitive powers have always proved to be better than a set of fortune-telling cards."

"Hey," George said irritably. "Are you two trying to spoil my day?"

"It won't be us spoiling anything for you," Track said. He waved his fork toward the towering Andes Mountains to the east. "The bastards that are going to do that are still waiting for you."

"For all of us," Zulu solemnly reminded both of them.

FELIPE'S GROUP MARCHED smartly up to the thatched barracks. They appreciated the coolness of early evening now that darkness had eased into Camp Oro. The yard in front of the oblong building was lit by gasoline lanterns hanging from the posts that supported the permanent wooden awnings sticking out from the building.

"Squad, halt!" the corporal bellowed.

The prisoners, who had begun drill earlier that day stumbling around each other, all came to a simultaneous, foot-stomping halt.

"Left, face!"

Felipe, bruised where the batons had been laid heavily across his buttocks and back, made a flawless turn.

"Behind you is your new home," the corporal announced. "The others in there have already eaten. You will have no meal tonight because you've done no work. But tomorrow you will begin the day with a big breakfast, and enter into the second in your series of training experiences. We are going to teach you a trade. When we have finished with you, all of you scum will be journeymen gold miners. Are you not grateful?"

"We thank the corporal!"

The corporal shook his head. "It is fortunate for you that Sergeant Zotol is not present to hear you bleat like sheep. But I am more merciful, and will forgive you—this time. When I dismiss you, you will go into the barracks directly behind you. Find an empty mat and make it yours. Mind what I say—an empty one! We'll not tolerate *aguas fescas* here that want to sleep with other men. Understood?"

"Yes, Corporal!"

"Very well. Squad, dis-missed!"

The formation melted away as the prisoners walked into the barracks to their rear. Felipe, in the middle of the crowd, stepped inside. He saw it was a narrow room with sleeping pallets of straw neatly arranged along the far wall. He wandered numbly down the row until he found an empty one. Exhausted, he immediately sank down on it.

"You'll get eating utensils tomorrow."

Felipe looked at the man situated next to him. "Pardon me?"

"I said you'll get a spoon and bowl tomorrow," the man said. "And a pair of shorts and sandals. Those will be your sole possessions here in Camp Oro.

Felipe looked down at the ripped remnants of his clothing. "Even that will be an improvement over what I have now."

The man smiled and offered his hand. "I am Antonio Poreso, at your service."

"Mucho gusto," Felipe said politely. "I am Felipe Rodriguez."

Poreso gestured at their surroundings. "For what it is worth, welcome to Camp Oro."

"I wish I were somewhere else," Felipe said.

"Tell me, amigo, what terrible sin did you commit to be sent to this awful place?" Poreso asked.

"I am a bandit," Felipe said. He grinned sheepishly. "Actually, I am a stupid bandit. I fell for a trick and got caught with a bunch of fellows from my home village. They killed most of them, and captured the rest of us."

"How adventurous," Poreso said. "My crime is that I am in Peru illegally. My home is in Mexico, in the state of Sinaloa. I came here because I heard there was gold to be found in the tributaries of the Amazon. I worked hard for six months and didn't find even an ounce of the stuff—but the soldiers found me. When they saw I had no proper papers, they arrested me." He laughed without humor. "Now, I have found gold." He pointed out the open door. "In that mine out there. The only trouble is, I must dig it out for others."

"Well," Felipe said, settling down on his mat, "don't worry, amigo. Do like that sign says. Work hard and earn your freedom. Then you'll see Mexico again."

Poreso glanced downward and clenched his teeth. "I have yet to see anyone get their release from this shithole."

Felipe sat up. He spoke in a worried tone. "How long have you been here?"

"Three years," Poreso said. "And I don't know for how much longer. When I used to enter the United States illegally, they simply bused me back home."

"I wonder how long they will keep me here for being a bandit," Felipe said.

"Our only chance for freedom will come through a deliverer—a messiah," Poreso said.

"You mean like *Jesucristo*?"

"Perhaps not quite that holy or divine. It will have to be some fellow that is tough enough to take on Zotol and Torres," Poreso said. He sighed. "Get some sleep, young friend. Tomorrow is going to be like all the other days—long and filled with hard labor and soldiers' rifle butts."

Felipe lay back and closed his eyes. Despite the fear and uncertainty he felt, he drifted off to sleep after only a short while.

He slept deeply and dreamlessly for three hours before he awoke again. The gasoline lanterns had been extinguished, and it was dark in the barracks. Felipe could hear the deep breathing of the other sleeping prisoners. He thought of his dead cousin Flaco, remembering how he had cursed and hit him when the poor, weak fellow had begged for help.

Shame and loathing for himself crept over Felipe. He rolled over and wept silently. It seemed that he was now being justly punished for the cruelty he'd shown Flaco. Then he remembered the poor lidless man staked out behind the huts.

Felipe prayed for the second time that day. He asked God for two things: forgiveness for being mean to Flaco; and someone, either angelic or mortal, to deliver him and the others from Camp Oro.

Although Felipe Rodriguez didn't know it, more than seven hundred kilometers away, a man named Dan Track was packing his bag for a journey that would come in the very direction where the young prisoner was held captive.

7

Track was back into his original rotten mood by the time their train arrived in Iquitos in late afternoon.

The journey had begun more than eighty hours earlier when Track and Company arrived at the Lima depot at a quarter to six in the morning. Their tickets, duly purchased and provided through The Consortium via the efforts of Mr. Horace Zindel, were presented at the gates. A railroad guard pointed them in the right direction, and they walked past several waiting trains to one that bore the proud name: *El Cometa*.

Even Track and George, not understanding Spanish, could figure out that particular appellation—The Comet. Despite the fact that the engine was an ancient steam job, its name still promised a rapid-as-lightning explosive journey across the Andes and down into the jungle country where Iquitos awaited them on the mighty Amazon River.

They boarded promptly with their bags and the wooden crate that supposedly held only geological survey tools. The three settled themselves into their compartment, ready for a quick departure.

At this point, with the thought of ascending into the famous mountain range of South America—and with his recent coupling with the sexy Ana Garanta still freshly stamped in his memory and on his loins—Dan Track was in an acceptable humor.

After carefully checking out the security of their location, the three comrades arranged the crate so that the weaponry inside could be reached in the case of any emergency. Then they set up a rotation of guard duty so that one of them would be awake at all times.

After that, there was nothing to do but brace themselves for the expected acceleration of *El Cometa* as it streaked eastward to the Andes and the adventure that awaited them on the other side.

An hour passed.

Track left the compartment and looked up and down the platform. He could see other passengers, some of them Indians in colorful costumes, boarding the train with a miscellaneous array of baggage. He stepped down from the car to get a better view of all that *El Cometa* encompassed. Aside from the engine and coal car, there was a baggage car and three passenger coaches. Only one, in which he and his friends were riding, seemed first class. The other two were crude and battered with only half the windows sporting any glass. Track also noted that some very unsavory and down-at-heel passengers were seated on the roofs of the coaches.

Track returned to his seat. "Looks like we'll be leaving pretty quick," he announced to Zulu and George. "There're people hopping on in a continual stream."

Two and a half hours rolled by.

Zulu, seeing the conductor, signaled to him through the glass. The august official opened the door and stuck his head in. *"¿Sí, señor?"*

"¿Cuándo vamos a salir?" Zulu asked.

"Muy pronto, señor," the conductor said. He closed the door and hurried off to his myriad of duties.

Zulu settled back. "He said we'd be leaving very soon."

Track checked his watch. "Christ! It's almost nine thirty."

George, not being required to stay awake, yawned and made himself comfortable. Within a few moments he was fast asleep.

Another two hours crawled by.

Track, angry now, started to get up and search out the conductor. Even if the son of a bitch couldn't understand English, he'd damned well know he had a real pissed-off passenger on his hands. Track opened the door, then stopped. "Shit!"

"What's the matter, Dan?" Zulu asked.

"I just remembered something," Track said. "Zindel told us the train would leave when it was filled." He returned to his seat. "I forgot we're in the land of *mañana*."

"I thought that was Mexico," George said, coming awake.

"It is any place in Latin America," Zulu said. "And who can argue with these good people? Perhaps that is the best philosophy to live by."

"If the rest of the world would adopt it, the coronary death rate would be halved," Track surmised. "But I'll be damned if much work would get done."

Finally, at three o'clock that afternoon, *El Cometa* had got her steam up and rolled slowly out of Lima to begin the climb into the towering mountain range that stood between the capital city and the steaming jungles.

Now, after a tedious journey that included countless delays and stops along the route, Track led his two friends out of the Iquitos depot to the street to get a cab. It was already getting dark. Evenings were short in this part of the world where the sun was quickly swallowed up by the towering mountains to the west.

Their crate of "geological tools," while not overly large, was big enough that the taxi driver couldn't close the trunk. The man, anxious to haul the *norteamericanos* and earn a generous tip, happily produced a short length of rope to secure the wooden box.

Track watched carefully as the driver deftly arranged the load. He happened to glance toward the depot and, once again, he saw the little man in the soiled white suit. Track quickly nudged Zulu. "Look!"

"At what?" Zulu asked, glancing around.

"Hell, he's gone," Track said. "It was that little fucker in the white suit again."

George eyed his uncle incredulously. "You mean the one from Lima? Are you sure you're not cracking up, Dan?"

"You two keep your eyes open," Track told them.

"Perhaps you're mistaken, Dan," Zulu suggested. "It's getting dark rather rapidly."

"I saw him, no doubt about it," Track insisted.

George followed him around the taxi as they got in. "There's lots o' little guys in white suits in South America."

"This is the same one," Track stated flatly.

The driver slid in behind the wheel. He looked back at them and grinned, speaking in his best English. "Hey, buddies, where to you want go, huh?"

"The docks on the river," Track answered.

"Okay, buddies, what of the boats you going to ride on?"

Zulu quickly checked their tickets. "It is *Estrella del Río*."

"Okay, buddies, here we go." The driver started the cab and raced out into traffic without so much as a preliminary glance. He immediately leaned on the horn.

Track grimaced. "What's the name of that boat?"

"*Estrella del Río,*" Zulu answered. "It means the *Star of the River*."

George laughed. "Oh, God! First we had the *Comet* that moved like molasses in January, and now we got the *Star of the River*. What do you want to bet it's a leaky, rusty tub with a fucked-up motor run by a drunken captain who hasn't looked at his watch in the past five years—if he has one."

Track sighed. "I just want to get this job done, and get the hell out of here."

In fifteen minutes, with the horn still blasting, the cab pulled up to one of several docks located on a wide river.

George, getting out of the taxi, whistled in amazement. "My God! You can't see the other side."

Zulu joined him. "That's the Amazon, young fellow. As famous as the Nile or Mississippi—but ten times more dangerous."

Track paid the cabbie, giving him a big tip despite the business with the horn. After unloading the crate, Track looked around to see where they should go, glancing across the street at a block of warehouses.

The little man in white stood between two of them. He was barely visible in the dull glow cast by a nearby streetlight.

"You two stay here," Track said.

"Where the hell are you going?" George asked, puzzled.

Track's voice was flat. "It's showdown time."

FELIPE RODRIGUEZ NUMBLY HUNG on to the scoop shovel as he walked forward in the line of convict miners. He didn't know where he was going or why. Someone had blown a whistle and barked orders to form a single file. After hours of muscle-grinding labor of scooping dirt into wheelbarrows, Felipe had only obeyed without thinking, thankful for a break in the hard work.

The line continued moving until he found himself outside the mine. Then he saw that it was evening and everyone was turning in their tools to a clerk. An armed soldier, ready for any badass who might decide a shovel or pick would make an excellent weapon, stood by. Felipe dropped off the digging utensil, then followed the others over to a long table.

There he received a palm frond folded into a crude, oblong bowl. It was filled with steamed fish, and there was some jungle fruit thrown on top. After being given a gourd of cold water, he wandered off to find a place to sit down.

"Here, Felipe Rodriguez. There is a spot by me." It was Antonio Poreso, the Mexican he'd met the night before.

Felipe squatted down. He now realized how famished he was. He scooped up some fish in his hands and began to eat. After swallowing the first mouthful, he slowed down. "At least they give you plenty to eat," he said.

Poreso nodded. "True, young friend. They want to keep you strong so you can work. But, beware! If you are injured or become sick, you will be disposed of quickly."

Felipe suddenly recalled how the corporal had explained Flaco's death to Sergeant Zotol. The soldier had said there had been no loss in Flaco's death—that he was sickly and coughed blood. Felipe sipped the cool, delicious water. "I shall not get sick then."

"Good. Even if you feel a little down, never show it," Poreso advised. "They look for that—and limping or favoring an arm or hand. Be careful."

"Thank you," Felipe said.

"How did this first day go for you?" Poreso asked.

Felipe shrugged. "Another fellow used a pick and dug out dirt from the wall of the mine. I scooped it into wheelbarrows that others pushed away. I didn't understand what I was doing."

"There is gold in that soil," Poreso explained. "Those fellows with the wheelbarrows take it out to the big trough. Water washes the dirt away but the gold, which is heavier, stays behind. It is taken away to somewhere else where it is melted down." He became thoughtful. "It seems rather inefficient. Most mines use cars on tracks instead of wheelbarrows, and they have other machinery, too." He sighed. "Ah, *bien*! Perhaps it is designed to keep the prisoners working as hard as possible."

"I think so," Felipe agreed. He looked around. "Now what do we do?"

"We are required to stay within this immediate vicinity until the soldiers make us go to bed," Poreso said.

"Are there no women here?" Felipe asked.

"They bring in prostitutes for the soldiers," Poreso said. "And Colonel Torres has a beautiful mistress that comes to visit him from time to time. I have seen her up close while I was on a work detail at the soldiers' barracks once."

Although the hard physical labor had exhausted him, and Felipe had no desire for a woman at that moment, he knew that soon he would. "What about us?"

"None for us," Poreso said bitterly. "They want all our physical strength to go for working. But one time a soldier got mad at a whore for something. He threw her in here. A lot of the fellows rushed for the woman. They had fights between themselves before they all took her. The poor thing died from it all." He lowered his voice and leaned forward. "There are men in here who are like wild animals. And this life doesn't improve their dispositions."

Felipe said nothing. He'd already sensed that he faced as much danger from some of his fellow prisoners as he did from Sergeant Zotol and the soldiers.

He shivered involuntarily, then went back to eating. Felipe wanted to keep up his strength.

TRACK HURRIED INTO THE CROWD around the steamship docks and made his way down toward the end. After reaching the edge of the debarkation area, he slipped into the darkness, then turned and raced across the street behind the warehouses.

He pulled the Beretta from the shoulder holster and hurried back in the direction from which he'd come. When he reached the right spot, he stopped and peered around the corner of the warehouse.

The little man in white stood there with his back to him. From the way the short fellow was glancing back and forth, Track knew the man was looking for him. The American eased around the corner and silently approached his quarry.

Track reached out and quickly grabbed him by the back of his shirt collar, pulling him rapidly backward into the darkness while pressing the automatic into the side of Shorty's head.

Track's voice was low and menacing. "Don't piss me off, or I'll splatter your fucking brains all over this wall."

The little guy, no more than five feet, six inches tall, hissed in fury. "Let me go!"

"Control yourself, my man," Track said. He stopped and spun him around, pushing him against the nearest warehouse. In the dull light coming in from the street, Track could see a pasty-faced European-type, with overly large eyes. The nose was small and puglike, while his mouth, thick-lipped and pouting, was formed into a snarl.

The little fellow, so furious his eyes bugged out farther, lost control. He impetuously grabbed Track's gun wrist with both hands and shook as hard as he could. "Oh—oh!" he sputtered, "I'll—kill you—you bastard—no good—stinking—goddamned bastard—"

Track grinned and grabbed the little man's throat with his free hand and began to pound his head against the wall. "Okay, shit-for-brains, I'll calm you down."

But Shorty's fury only grew until he was frothing at the mouth. Unable to form words, he growled and spit in rage.

Track ended the tirade by hitting him solidly with an open hand.

The man fell to the ground, holding his face. But his tantrum was abating. "You—you—you!"

Track smiled. "Yes?"

Shorty panted in anger, then even that subsided. He swallowed and spit. "The Inca sun shines always."

"Say, what?" Track inquired.

The little man glared at him. "Idiot! I said, 'The Inca sun shines always.'"

Then Track remembered the recognition signal given him by Horace Zindel. He replied, "As long as its people live." Then he stepped back.

"You are Dan Track," the short fellow said, getting to his feet. He brushed off his already dirty coat and trousers.

"As they say in melodramas, you have the advantage," Track said.

"My name is Hessler—Don Juan Hessler. Why did you attack me like a common thug?"

Track noted he spoke with an unidentifiable accent that hovered somewhere between Latin American and German. He parried the question with one of his own. "Why have you been following me, Hessler? Don't you think it would have been wiser to have approached me sooner?"

"If I had thought so, I would have done it," Hessler said. "There's no time for stupid chatter. Let's get moving. We must get aboard that boat for the ten o'clock sailing. I shall meet you and your friends in the salon later. Wait for me there." He hurried off across the street toward the dock.

Track reholstered the Beretta, then followed. He joined Zulu and George. "Let's get our stuff and board."

"What's going on, Dan?" George asked.

"I'll explain later," Track said. "But my feelings of foreboding for this mission have just jumped tenfold."

The three gathered their baggage and walked to the boarding ramp of the *Estrella del Río*.

8

George Beegh's gloomy prediction about the condition of the riverboat called the *Estrella del Río* was not completely accurate—but it was close.

The boat, down at heel by any standards, made up for its surface shabbiness by having an engine kept in top running condition through the efforts of a brutal captain who kept his crew in line with his fists and boots. The deck might be worn, and there were screens missing from some of the cabin doors and windows, but the steam-piston machinery that drove the paddle wheel was oiled, wiped and in excellent repair. The men who serviced her were a couple of sweaty, unwashed specimens who should have tended to their own personal cleanliness with the same meticulous care they showed the power plant of the *Estrella del Río*.

The cabin occupied by Track and Company would not have rated a single star in any tourist booklet. But it was clean. There was a pair of bunks stacked along one bulkhead and a single bed on the other side. Zulu, the first to enter the cabin, rushed for the single bed without hesitation. He sat down on his prize, and displayed a happy smile to his two companions. "There is a rather basic and simple philosophy about there being two sorts of people in the world," he said, explaining his action, "the quick and the hungry. I therefore claim this single berth in the spirit of that school of thought."

Track immediately tossed his bag across the room onto the bottom bunk. He grinned at George. "Any questions?"

George's only remark as he stood motionless and outplayed was a single word. "Shit!"

Five minutes later Track and George were stowing away their gear while Zulu tended to patching up the screen in their cabin door. Being from the tropics, he knew full well the importance of keeping a tight barrier between oneself and insects—particularly those whose bites could cause sickness.

Track slid his bag under the bunk in their cramped quarters. "By the way, I guess you two will listen the next time I tell you that there's somebody shadowing us."

George grinned as he sat down on the cabin's one chair. "Especially if he's a little bitty fucker in a white suit."

Zulu, who had sewn up the rip in the screen using fishing line from the survival kit he always kept in his gear, finished the task and stepped back. "Gentlemen," he announced, "there's not a bug in all of South America that can get to us now."

"That's fine while we're aboard this tub," Track said, "but what about in the jungle?"

Zulu shrugged. "As a veteran of Vietnam, you know as well as I that, while outside of netting, you're meat on the hoof to any sort of biting creature, be it mosquito, blowfly or leech."

George shuddered. "God! You make my skin crawl!"

Track winked at him. "Want us to change the subject?"

"Sure," George said. "Let's talk about that little guy in the white suit."

"I'd rather talk about snakes," Track said.

"At any rate, he's the man we deal with," Zulu reminded him. Then he added, "Whether we like it or not."

"I just saw him for an instant when you two came back from across the street," George said. "He looked like a sneaky, underhanded, pint-size son of a bitch."

Zulu laughed. "You're certainly not extending the little chap any benefit of the doubt, are you?"

"Hell, no!" George exclaimed.

"I don't like him either," Track said. "I don't like the way he looks at you. It's as if he wants to sneer in your face, but doesn't really want it known what he thinks of you. That nasal voice of his doesn't add much to his charm either."

"Come now!" Zulu scoffed. "The little gentleman may well be a connoisseur of the arts or historical relics. He evidently had enough knowledge to contact the Peruvian National Museum about Pizarro's calendar, didn't he?"

"Yeah," Track agreed. "But he sure as hell didn't do it out of an altruistic or philanthropic concern to get a valuable display to a museum. This seems to be strictly business on his part."

"Sometimes," Zulu countered, "a certain set of circumstances can force a chap to be mercenary when he'd rather be a bit more of a gentleman."

"I'm with George," Track stated flatly. "I'm not giving the little bastard a shred of trust. Don't forget he didn't want to deal with any middlemen. That's us, my friends, and there's a damn good chance he'll try to waste us sometime between getting the calendar and returning to Lima."

"We shall see, shan't we?" Zulu said.

Track checked his watch. "And very quickly, too. It's time we went to the salon."

George took note of the hot, muggy air in the cabin. "A cold beer sounds great."

"Shall we?" Zulu asked.

"Let's," Track said, leading the way out the door. He waited outside as his two companions joined him. Then he took the padlock he normally used on his valise and pulled the main cabin door closed and secured it. "Any thieves could go through this after ripping through the screen door, but it's better than nothing."

"It's the only choice we have unless one of us stays behind," George said.

Track shook his head. "I want us all in that salon. Once I'm satisfied that everything is on the up-and-up I'll send you two back one at a time to take turns guarding our stuff."

"I suggest we don't leave the cabin untended for any more than fifteen minutes," Zulu said. "Can we check things out that fast?"

"We'll have to," Track said. He tapped George. "You'll take the first turn."

"Right," George said. He noted the time. "In fifteen minutes I'll melt away and come back here."

Their cabin was on the lower of two decks. They took the stairs and went directly to the salon, which was located in the stern. They found the place to be a bit primitive, but the bar had running water and a small refrigerator to keep beer and soft drinks cold. The view to the aft was beautiful, a panorama of the Amazon River and the thick jungle that crowded right up to the water's edge.

There were no other patrons in the salon except a sleepy Latin American who dozed at a table with a drink growing warm in front of him. Track and Company took a table off to one side. From there they had a full view of the room and the two entrance and exit doors.

The barman shouted over to them. *"Si ustedes queréis algo, tenéis que venir aquí. No soy mesero."*

Zulu waved in acknowledgment, then turned to his companions. "He says if we want something we'll have to go up there. He's not a table waiter."

Track nudged George. "I'll have a beer."

George raised his eyebrows. "Why certainly. Ol' handy George is always around to jump up and fetch things, right?"

"Right," Zulu said. "A gin and tonic for me. Sir Abner says it's the perfect drink for the tropics."

"Jeez!" George complained. But he got up and went to the bar.

George had to drink his beer quickly before his scheduled stint as guard in the cabin began. "What do we call this," he complained, "Fuck George Week? First I end up on the top bunk, and now I have to run errands, and stand the first watch, too."

Track laughed. "Now you got it!" Then he added, "And speaking of guard duty—"

George tipped his head back and drained the bottle. "See you two generous bastards later." He hurried off.

A few seconds later Don Juan Hessler came into the salon.

He walked across the room to their table in a manner that could best be described as a haughty waddle. Rather than utter a greeting, he asked a question. "That young man who just left—is he with you?"

"Yes," Track said.

Hessler sat down at the table. He turned and snapped his fingers at the bartender. "Bacardi!"

The man reached behind the bar and produced a bottle of the famous rum and a glass. He poured a serving, then called back. *"Aquí está."*

Hessler's brows dived into a frown. *"¡Traimelo!"*

"No soy mesero, venga para su traigo."

Hessler leaped to his feet, his small plump body shaking in rage. *"¡Traimelo inmediatamente!"*

The bartender shot him a defiant look, then shrugged. He walked over and set the drink down. He salvaged his pride by sneering at the little man, then returned to the bar.

Hessler calmed down as quickly as he had become enraged. He turned his full attention to Track. "Let's get down to business, shall we?"

"You're calling the shots, Hessler," Track said. "By the way, my friend here is—"

Hessler interrupted him. "Hodari Zulu. Yes, I know. And the other fellow is George Beegh." He took a sip of the rum. "Now here is what we are to do. We will leave the boat at Rio Vista. That is a small town to the east. From there we will get a couple of launches and go up the Riachuelo Verde—that is a small tributary of the Amazon. Somewhere up that small river, we will find the man who will give us Pizarro's calendar."

"How far up?" Track asked.

Hessler shrugged. "I don't know. My client is a crude man who lives in the jungle. After he has fouled a campsite so much that even he can't stand it, he moves on. But he has assured me we will have no trouble finding him."

"What's his name?" Track asked.

"That is something I shall keep to myself," Hessler said. "But I will share a certain amount of knowledge with you. I have four men who will accompany us."

"Where are they?"

"You will meet them soon," Hessler said.

"Parade 'em past us-right now," Track said grimly.

Hessler sneered. "You will meet them when—"

"Get 'em in here or the deal's off."

Hessler's temper flared, making his eyes bulge as he gritted his teeth. "Don't dictate to me, Track!"

Track leaned forward, keeping his voice cold and businesslike. "Not only is the deal off, but I'll throw your pudgy ass into the fucking Amazon."

"You are going to go too far!" Hessler hissed. "I will not tolerate threats or bullying from you—" he turned his glare on Zulu "—or you!"

"Get your men in here so I can take a look at them," Track insisted. "And if any others show up during this undertaking, I'll waste 'em. Understand?"

Hessler was trembling by then. But within a couple of minutes, the tantrum subsided. He stood up. "If you insist on being difficult, there is nothing I can do. Wait here."

Track went to the bar and got himself another beer. By the time he returned to the table, Hessler was back. The little man resumed his seat. "Thc first onc is coming in now."

A burly Latin American, sporting black curly hair and a gigantic mustache, walked into the bar. He stayed away from the table. After getting a drink, he walked over to the stern and nonchalantly stared out at the river.

"That is Rafael," Hessler said.

Another man sauntered through the door and up to the bar. He stayed there, sipping the beer he had ordered. He was tall, skinny, and sported a short-cropped beard.

"That is Laredo," Hessler informed Track and Zulu.

Within five minutres, there were two more. Hessler identified them as Pedro and Francisco.

Track quickly made his demand. "Get rid of two of them."

"What?" Hessler asked in shock.

"You heard what I said," Track said, getting up. "There will be three of us—and three of you."

Hessler's disposition went sour again. "You—you—don't tell me—"

"Get rid of 'em, or the deal is off," Track said. He quickly walked away from the table with Zulu following.

Hessler leaped to his feet and spun around. He started to shout something at Track, but he choked off the words. Instead, the little man stood there shaking in fury. When he finally spoke, his voice trembled in hateful anger.

"I am going to kill that arrogant bastard!"

DON JUAN HESSLER WAS BORN in Lima, Peru, in 1942. His father, Dietrich Hessler, had entered the country illegally several years before, after being released from prison in Germany. He had been convicted and sentenced to five years' confinement for embezzlement and fraud as a partner in a beer-brewing firm in Munich.

He had originally gone into the business with two other master brewers. A smattering of accountant's training had earned him the title of company treasurer. He looted the firm outrageously while, at the same time, keeping such a confusing set of books that it took an entire staff of financial investigators to determine finally that charges were appropriate. But the case was finally brought to trial and Dietrich Hessler went behind bars.

After release from prison he found his wife had left him. With no real reason to stay in Germany, Dietrich Hessler arranged for a forged passport from a former cellmate. He sincerely desired to start a new life, and like many Germans, he found something about South America attracted him.

He arrived in Peru in 1936 with the idea of starting up his own brewery. Dietrich dreamed of the day that Hessler Beer would make him wealthy as all of Latin America adopted it.

But without money—or the right connections—his goal seemed unattainable. The best job he could find was in a travel agency. It was a prosperous business with offices in all of Peru's largest cities. Dietrich, in desperation, made a move he thought was probably useless—a play to marry the boss's daughter.

The German, used to Europe's class distinction between employee and employer, didn't think he'd stand a chance. But he thought the reward for success warranted at least a damned serious try. To his surprise, he was accepted, thanks to a sort of reverse racism practiced by the locals.

Many wealthy Latin American families with a strong Indian lineage desired to breed that part of the heritage away. In a land where marriages were arranged, the patriarch always made sure his offspring mated with Europeans or at least with people whose mestizo mixture was mostly white. Dietrich Hessler was exactly the type his employer was searching for as a son-in-law. The blond, blue-eyed German seemed the perfect way to ensure that the grandchildren had white characteristics.

An arrangement was made, and Dietrich Hessler became the husband of Isabel Gloria Sanchez-Franco. She was plump, unattractive, short and boring. But her papa had money, and Hessler was able to act like an enthusiastic bridegroom.

Dietrich invested his wife's generous dowry in a beer-brewing enterprise. The man might have been a crook, but he was a master brewer and he practiced his craft faithfully, producing a superior product that sold well from the start.

The only child of the marriage was Don Juan. Dietrich himself chose the name. His wife's argument that the word "Don" was a title of knighthood like the word "Sir" in English did not deter the man. He'd read of the great lover and adventurer Don Juan, and wanted his son—who was sure to grow into a tall Germanic swashbuckler—to bear that proud and significant name.

But Don Juan Hessler did not live up to his sire's expectations. The fat little boy had his father's coloring and his mother's tendency toward shortness. And to add to his homeliness, he inherited all of the least attractive characteristics of both bloodlines.

As he grew older and it became obvious that he would not blossom, the father turned his full attention to his business enterprise and ignored his son as much as possible. When Dietrich did speak to Don Juan, he always did so in German. Thus the boy, while speaking fluent, faultless Spanish, developed a strange speech pattern. His accent vacillated somewhere between Spanish and German, with a sort of nasal twang thrown in.

The brewery prospered and, with it, the family. This good luck was well timed, since Grandpa Sanchez's travel business failed during a massive devaluation of the Peruvian sol.

It was characteristic of Dietrich to offer no help to his father-in-law. He let the old man and his wife endure poverty while living on the handouts their daughter managed to wrest from her husband's tight fists.

But none of this had an effect on Don Juan. He went to private schools where he displayed a quick intelligence but a quicker Teutonic temper. He was constantly getting into fights brought on by his enormous tantrums. Since he was a better baiter than brawler he was always beaten to a pulp, but none of these unlucky encounters did a thing to curb his rages.

Then the bottom fell out of his life.

Dietrich Hessler had kept close contact with the old country. During the Second World War he had been a hard-nosed Nazi sympathizer. When that conflict came to a close, he turned his efforts to aiding Nazi war criminals to enter Peru illegally. Finally, one of the men he was helping was spotted by agents of the newly created state of Israel.

The Jewish avengers made plans to kidnap the fugitive. The action went down on a busy street corner. Dietrich Hessler happened to be with the target of the agents. In the ensuing gunfight a couple of rounds from a British surplus Sten gun smashed into Dietrich's skull, ending his life.

The widow Hessler had no head for commerce. Her father, a sound businessman, had died a year previously. Thus, the brewery went to hell without the German master brewer's iron hand. Little Don Juan, then twelve years old, was taken from private school. The family home was lost and mother and son were forced to move to some rather unfashionable suburbs.

Don Juan, who had had trouble getting along with his rich playmates, found the poorer ones intolerable. His school life was a series of disasters and he finally left school at the age of sixteen.

He drifted onto the streets where crime was rampant. Too small and delicate to be a strong-arm thief, Don Juan developed a subtle talent for the sneakier side of underworld activities: he picked pockets, rolled drunken sailors, fleeced tourists and finally moved into a one-man operation where he became an errand boy for white-collar criminals who deal in stolen objets d'art, phony stocks and securities and other con games.

His life ricocheted through a series of ups and downs. He either had plenty of money and a fancy apartment where the closets were stuffed with the best and most elegant clothing available in Lima, or he was completely busted—broke, hungry and meaner than hell.

When he made the contact that led to the deal for Pizarro's calendar, he was at bottom—and Don Juan Hessler was willing to do anything necessary to get back to the top of the heap.

9

The *Estrella del Río*, her paddle wheel thrown into reverse, eased toward the dock in Rio Vista.

Crewmen tossed heavy lines to waiting dockhands, who quickly and expertly whipped the ropes around the wharf's posts. The big riverboat strained against them, then finally settled down to bump against the old rubber tires attached to the dock's edge. There was a brief silence when the engine was cut. It was soon filled with the happy babbling of passengers and those who had come to greet them.

The landing crew quickly slid the loading ramp up to the deck railing where the exit gate was located.

Disembarking passengers, eager to get ashore, hurried down the ramp. But Dan Track, Hodari Zulu and George Beegh stayed on the lower deck with their baggage and the crate holding the surveying instruments and firearms. They stood without talking, each quietly and efficiently keeping a sharp eye on his particular zone of security.

George had fashioned a hinged affair in the box that could be wrenched loose by hand, offering quick access to the SPAS-12 shotgun, the AR-15 and the Uzi, which were packed close together. The intrepid young man sat down on the box, his legs straddling the well-hidden door. He could meet any emergency by quickly flipping the crate open, then tossing out their individual weapons to his two friends. Then he would bring his own AR-15 9-millimeter into whatever play had occurred.

But nothing more exciting happened than Don Juan Hessler showing up with his gunmen, Rafael and Laredo, in tow. He pointed to his other two men, who stood sullenly by the rail amidships. "I have agreed to your terms, Track," Hessler said with his strange nasal accent. "That pair stays. Thus, as you so stubbornly insisted, we are three each."

Track smiled sarcastically. "Six happy travelers, right, Hessler?"

Hessler did not rise to the bait. "We won't be doing any traveling at all until I make arrangements for launches to take us up the Riachuelo Verde." He paused and sneered. "Unless you don't trust me to accomplish that without concocting some sort of treacherous plot against you and your two companions."

Track's smile faded. "Let's get one thing straight. You pull any shit—you die."

Hessler's face paled in anger. "Don't threaten me! I won't be intimidated by your vulgar street talk, Track. You may not be aware of it, but you owe me and several of my men a great deal."

"I'm aware you eased the situation in front of the hotel the day the urban guerrillas fired on the limousine we were riding in," Track interjected. "And, I might add, I've made you hanging around the area on several occasions." He grinned and pointed to Zulu and George. "Although these two sharp-eyed jokers didn't see you."

Hessler's bug eyes widened even a bit more. "You are a very alert man, Track. Still, let me warn you, I do not appreciate threats."

"Then don't think of my remarks as threats, Hessler," Track said. "Regard them as promises—sacred promises."

"You idiot!" Hessler hissed under his breath as his control again slipped. "You stupid imbecile! Do you think I would betray you? It is imperative to me that we get Pizarro's calendar back to Lima as quickly as possible. Why do you insist on playing out this melodramatic game of deception and suspicion?"

"Intuition," Track said. "Plus the fact I know you don't really want the three of us along on this ride."

It took a full minute for Hessler to regain complete control of his temper. When his emotions had cooled somewhat, he even attempted a smile of sorts. "See here, Track. We'll get nowhere with belligerent attitudes. We should all be comrades. Particularly when you consider the fact we will be going into the heart of bandit country. I suggest we turn our hostilities toward the very real threat we face there." The little man stopped smiling. "Unless you're not worried, of course. Tell me, Track. Do you consider yourself the toughest, meanest man in the world?"

"Of course not," Track said. Then he grinned. "But, y'know, that son of a bitch keeps calling me up trying to make friends."

"Clever comeback, Track," Hessler replied. He motioned to Rafael and Laredo to leave the boat. Then he snapped his attention back to Track. "Meet me at that bar located on the end of the dock. I will be there within two or three hours."

"Please hurry," George said from his seat on the crate. "Every moment will seem like an eternity."

"¡Yanquis arrogantes!" Hessler strode down the gangplank and onto the wharf.

Zulu watched the South American disappear into the crowd on the dock. "Do not underestimate the little fellow," he remarked. "I judge him to be quite dangerous if pushed too far."

"You're right," Track said. "But he's such a cocky gnome that he brings out my worst qualities."

"Piss on him," George said. "Let's get our stuff and get on down to that bar." He wiped at the perspiration on his face. "Christ! Not even midmorning and it's hotter'n hell already."

The trio put their personal baggage on top of the crate and carried it off the boat and down to the street. The crude avenue, wide and unpaved, was bordered by various businesses that were designed to cater to river travelers. Most were operated out of structures so sparse and crude that the enterprises could best be described as "open air."

Track, Zulu and George walked to a crude saloon that sported a thatched roof. The interior of the establishment was far from fancy, but it was functional. A long bar made of planks dominated one side of the small building. A half-dozen battered tables and chairs were crowded into the remainder of the place.

Track and Company set their things down at the bar. There were four other men drinking in the place. They gave the newcomers only cursory glances, then went back to their lethargic imbibing.

Track waved to the bartender and raised three fingers. "*Tres* beers," he said. Then he grinned at Zulu. "How's that for Spanish?"

"Not bad, Dan," Zulu said.

The saloon keeper, displaying a gap-toothed grin beneath an ill-kept handlebar mustache, set three bottles of beer on the bar. "That's pretty good," he said in well-spoken but accented English. "Now all you got to do is learn the word for beer. And that's *cerveza*."

"Right," Track said in a friendly tone. *"Tres cervezas."*

"What part o' the States you from?" the barman asked.

"Ohio," Track lied. He pointed to Zulu. "Except him—he's from Canada."

The man offered his hand. "I'm Diego Beldaro—that's Jim Beldaro in English, so you can call me Jimmy, eh?"

"Glad to know you, Jimmy," Track said. "I'm Dan and this is Hodari and George."

"You speak excellent English," Zulu said, picking up his cold beer.

"Thank you," Jimmy said, genuinely pleased. "I lived for a long time in Colorado. But I didn't have no papers and one day a guy who wanted my job squealed. The immigration agents came and hauled me away."

"Too bad," Track said.

"Sure. I had a fine job in construction. Made good dough, too," Jimmy said. "I got out with enough to open up this little place. It ain't much, but it's a living."

George looked around. "Maybe you should have gone into business in a bigger place. Like Lima or Iquitos."

"Normally I would have," Jimmy explained. "But I do a lot of investing around here."

"Really?" Zulu asked. "May I ask in what?"

"Gold," Jimmy said. "I'm what you American guys call a grubstaker. I give prospectors some equipment and food to take out into the jungle. Later they come back with a few nuggets and I get a cut. A little at a time, but it's mounting up."

"There's gold in this part of the world?" George asked.

"You bet!" Jimmy said. "Somewhere out here is a big mine—maybe even more than one. They say the old Indians—the Incas—had 'em here. Them bastards used slaves to dig the ore outta the ground for them."

"Could be just legends," Track said.

"Yeah," George said, echoing his feelings. "Legends and bullshit."

Jimmy shook his head. "No way, man. Them ancients had lots o' gold trinkets and stuff. There wasn't no gold on the other side o' the Andes, man. That shit's out here somewhere, and I'm gonna find the mother lode myself someday."

Zulu grinned. "Want to be a wealthy man, hey?"

"You bet!" Jimmy suddenly laughed. "I'll go back to Colorado and buy that construction comp'ny. Then I'll fire that son of a bitch who took my job away."

One of the bar patrons interrupted the conversation. *"¡Ya vienen los soldados!"* he called out.

Jimmy glanced outside, then bent close to Track and Company. He spoke in a whisper. "You guys cool it, eh? There's three soldiers coming this way."

"So what?" Track asked.

"It's a patrol, man, and they'll give you a ration of crap," Jimmy said with a serious expression. "Just don't talk back, that's all."

"Fuck 'em," George said angrily.

"It's hard for Americans to put up with that kind o' stuff," Jimmy implored, "but, for God's sake, watch it! They'll haul your asses away to jail."

Track nudged George. "Cool it, understand?"

"Aw, hell!"

"Goddammit, George!"

"All right, Dan, all right! I won't mouth off," George promised.

Track took time to check out the other customers in the bar. They seemed preoccupied with their drinks, showing a great deal of interest in the glass mugs, keeping their eyes downcast. He turned to the door in time to see three husky soldiers in camouflage uniforms stride in. They were sharp dudes, looking tough and disciplined.

They stopped at the nearest table where a solitary man sat. Some shouting in Spanish followed, then the unlucky customer was yanked from his seat and shoved hard against the wall. His papers were pulled from his pocket by one soldier while a second whipped the civilian around and slapped him hard in the face. The third soldier, his French submachine gun slung loosely over his shoulder, had turned to face the other people in the saloon.

After five minutes it became obvious that the man's papers were in order. The soldier, however, kept bullying the citizen with a lecture as he punctuated the points he wished to make with hard jabs to the guy's chest.

It was easy to see their victim was cowed, helpless in the face of threats of arrest.

The three soldiers finally left the man and turned their attention to the bar where Track and Company stood. They strode over the short distance across the little saloon. The first soldier pointed to the crate. *"¿Qué es esto?"*

Track, thinking of the weapons inside, swallowed hard.

The soldier stepped forward and kicked the crate. *"Les pregunte qué es esto. ¡Contestanme!"*

Zulu stepped forward and sat one large foot on the crate. *"Son nuestros instrumentos, señor."*

Track listened to the ensuing conversation between Zulu and the military policeman. He was only able to pick up one word that was similar in English: *geologico*. But he also caught the word *gringo* and *yanqui* in the soldier's guttural response. The way the words were used did not convey any friendliness.

Finally the soldier signaled for Zulu to shut up. He pointed to the crate. *"Abrela."*

Zulu looked at Track. "He wants us to open it."

Track gritted his teeth. "Shit!"

Suddenly one of the other soldiers stepped forward and pulled a short bayonet from a scabbard on his cartridge belt.

George paled slightly, afraid the trooper would find the hinged opening he'd made in the crate. But the soldier went to the opposite side and slid the blade between a couple of boards and pried. Nails gave way and one of the short planks popped open.

The first soldier reached inside and withdrew the papers that Dr. Cordoba had put in with the tools. He flipped the packet over and saw the wax seal of the Peruvian republic that held it together. It was easy to see that his mind was racing as he tried to decide what to do.

Zulu stepped forward. *"Estamos en un viaje de negocios para su gobierno, señor."* He looked over at Track. "I just told him we're on government business."

The soldier glanced at the papers one more time. Then he shrugged and dropped them back into the crate. *"Bien,"* he announced. After a quick glance around the bar, he motioned to his two men and led them back outside into the street.

Jimmy closed his eyes and took a deep, relieved breath. "It's a good thing them papers was in order."

Track watched George knock the loose board back into place. "What's the story on those guys? They were acting more like cops than soldiers."

"They're part of an elite paratrooper unit that's stationed here," Jimmy explained. "They spend most o' their time out in the boondocks, but come in here regular like to check on things. Hell, a coupla weeks ago they suckered in a bandit gang and did a job on 'em."

"Clever and mean, huh?" George said, turning his attention back to his beer.

"You bet!" Jimmy said. "They spread word that there was a bunch of caiman hides stored here in Rio Vista. They did it to tempt some greedy bastards—any greedy bastards—to make a raid. They were waiting. Like I said, they wasted 'em. And those they didn't kill, they took away."

"We're heading out into the jungle," Zulu said. "Do you suppose we shall meet with those paratroopers again?"

"Yeah," Jimmy said. "Either them or bandits—or both."

"Which is worse?" George asked.

"Hard to tell," Jimmy said. He noticed another customer was signaling to him. "I gotta go. I'll be back in a minute."

Track treated himself to another swallow of the cold beer. "This is turning out to be quite a mission. We'll be out in some of the worst wilderness in the world with tigers, poisonous snakes, gestapo paratroopers, bandits and Don Juan Hessler."

Zulu raised his bottle. "Here's to adventure, chaps."

George shook his head. "I like thrills and chills too, Zulu. But not by the fucking carload."

"Like it or not," Track said, "we're up to our eyeballs in it."

10

The hum of the battery-driven outboards on the two launches could barely be heard as the craft moved slowly against the current of the Riachuelo Verde, the small tributary that flowed into the mighty Amazon.

Track rode in the lead boat with Hessler and his henchman Laredo. The South American had discarded his white suit for a pair of light, khaki overalls. He wore boots and had a snub-nosed Smith & Wesson .38 revolver in a holster rig strapped around his waist. Laredo, manning the tiller of the minimotor propelling the boat, sported a Winchester Model 94 30-30 carbine to back up his boss.

Despite his city background, Hessler had chosen clothing and conducted himself in a way that made it was obvious he had spent at least a bit of time in the jungle.

Track and Company, always ready, were dressed in surplus U.S. Army jungle fatigues and boots. Their arms, which had previously been kept hidden in the trunk, were now in the open—locked and loaded.

The second boat, occupied by Zulu, George and Hessler's other man, Rafael, followed in the slow journey that penetrated deeper into the thick jungle.

Hessler kept a wary eye on their surroundings, constantly vigilant, taking in as much as possible. He finally looked back at George in the rear launch and grinned at him. "I wouldn't put my hand in the water, if I were you, Beegh," he said pleasantly.

George splashed the water. "Why not? Is a big ol' alligator going to bite it off?"

"A bit worse than that," Hessler said. He drew his revolver.

Track stiffened and brought up the muzzle of the SPAS-12 assault shotgun. "Easy, Hessler."

Hessler's face contorted into a frown. "No! You take it easy, Track. I am merely going to make a point." He aimed his pistol upward into a swarm of monkeys that screeched and scampered in the tangle of tree branches that arched over the river. Hessler pulled the trigger.

A screaming, small furry creature tumbled down from its leafy sanctuary and hit the water. It struggled weakly as its blood turned the muddy murk around it to a rust color.

Suddenly the animal screamed again as a churning mass surrounded it, kicking up red foam. Within seconds the disturbance subsided, and all was quiet again.

"That monkey," Hessler announced, "has been reduced to a skeleton that is now sinking slowly to the river bottom."

George stared at the spot in the water where the quick, violent death had taken place. "What the hell?"

"Piranha," Hessler explained. "The little fish with the big needle teeth that go about in large schools. They can reduce a full-grown cow to mere bones in less than a minute. Or—" he laughed loudly "—strip the flesh from some careless idiot's hand in only a second or two."

George quickly pulled his hand out of the water.

Track looked back at his nephew and winked. "You just reminded me of the story about the kid who was always hanging around the blacksmith shop. One day he accidentally picked up a hot horseshoe and threw it right back down. When the blacksmith asked him if he'd burned himself, the kid said, 'No. It just don't take me long to look at a horseshoe.' "

Even Hessler laughed aloud at the old joke.

George grinned sheepishly. "So it doesn't take me long to get my hand wet, huh?"

"Right," Zulu said with a wide smile.

George's mood sobered a bit. "Jungles suck, man."

"Yeah," Track agreed. "I found that out in Vietnam."

This was the second day of their journey. The previous night had been spent quite pleasantly on a wide sandbar in the middle of the Riachuelo Verde. The Spanish word *riachuelo* actually means creek. This was what the Verde had been formerly, but time and natural erosion had widened it until it was a deep, slowly moving river with a width that varied from twenty feet to as many meters. In some places it was deep enough to cover a full-grown man, while in others the travelers had to get out to drag their flat-bottomed launches through mere inches of water.

George, growing impatient, complained. "I wish to hell we had motors that were a trifle larger. Ever hear of a gasoline Evinrude, Hessler?"

"Too much noise and weight," Hessler said. "It pays to be as quiet as possible in bandit country."

George laughed. "Bandit country? Do you mean to tell me that there's a bunch of poor, dumb miserable bastards hanging around this river on the off chance that a bunch of fuckers like us will come boating through?"

"Not at all," Hessler said. "This is their home area; they live here between raids on towns and settlements. Do not try to fool yourself that they will allow us to pass safely through their midst if they happen to hear us."

Zulu, who had been dozing with his burly body stretched out comfortably, looked up. "Then I suggest that we practice a bit more noise discipline, chaps. In other words, there's far too much talking going on."

"Aw, hell, Zulu!" George scoffed. "You just want to sleep."

"I see nothing wrong in that," Zulu said, closing his eyes again.

"Your friend makes a good point," Hessler said. He looked at Laredo. "Do you think we're close to the *bandidos* yet?"

Laredo shrugged. "Not now, but sure thing in another day."

Rafael, guiding the rear boat, shook his head in disagreement. "One hour after we leave the Amazon, we're close to them."

Track shifted the Franchi shotgun. "Then how about everybody shutting the fuck up, huh? A little less yapping and a lot more listening might keep us from ending up as piranha food."

"I agree," Hessler said.

Track was as glad as Zulu for the quiet. He wasn't sleepy though. His head—and heart—were filled again with thoughts of Desiree Goth. He tried to smother the sentimental onslaught by mentally reliving the wild night he'd spent with Ana Garanta, but no matter how sensuous and wild his recollections became, he always drifted back to memories of the woman he loved.

Track knew he had to discipline himself in order to regain his self-control. This called for a great deal of concentration, and the constant yammering between Hessler and George was distracting.

Then something even more disturbing occurred.

An ambush exploded from the riverbank to their left. Hot metal zapped through the air and small geysers of water erupted around the launches from the bullets hitting the river.

Rafael summed up the situation with one wild Spanish cry:

"*¡Emboscada!*" Ambush!

FELIPE RODRIGUEZ and the other prisoners of Camp Oro's convict brigade stood motionless in steady unwavering ranks as the hot sun pounded down on them. Angry, frustrated soldiers wielding mahogany batons beat and kicked the captives as a painstaking head count was conducted for the fifth time. This final effort, like all the others, ended with the senior corporal reporting loud and clear to Sergeant Zotol: "One man missing!"

"What unit?" Zotol demanded.

"Third Squad, Second Company."

"Send the men to work," Zotol commanded. "Except the Third Squad of the Second Company."

"Yes, *mi sargento*!" The order was given, and the other platoons of convict-laborers marched off to their various work assignments. Nine men were left standing in the sun. Among them was Felipe Rodriguez.

Zotol approached the men. If he was angry—and there was no doubt he was—he kept it hidden. He counted slowly. "In the organization plan of Camp Oro there are supposed to be ten men in a squad. Yet I only count nine."

The men tensed.

"Perhaps I miscounted," Zotol suggested. "I shall do it again." He walked up to the first man in the ranks and hit him hard. "One!" The second received the same. "Two!" And the third, "Three!"

Felipe was number seven. He closed his eyes as the big fist caught him on the mouth and nostrils. He staggered backward, barely able to keep his balance. But, despite his dizziness and pain, he rushed back to his proper place in the ranks. The punch to the face was bad enough—a kick to the testicles for not being dressed properly was even worse.

Zotol continued his count. "Eight! Nine!" Then he went back to the front of the small unit. "So, I did not make a mistake. There are only nine of you. One of the curs is missing. And you—all of you—were in on his escape!"

Felipe, who had never spoken to the missing man, could barely recall what the fugitive even looked like.

"So we are going to talk to you about him," Zotol said. He motioned to the corporal, then walked away. The soldier took command of the squad and marched them across the camp to the place where the little houses with the small windows stood out in the open. Each of the prisoners was led to one. After being ordered to strip off their shorts and sandals, the naked men were pushed inside.

Felipe had hardly managed to turn around in the cramped space when the door slammed shut. There was a small slit a foot long and no more than an inch high across the locked portal. Felipe pressed his eye against it to look out, but could see nothing but an empty part of the prison grounds.

The heat built up fast inside the confines of the standing box, and Felipe's body reacted. Within a few moments he was soaking wet with the warm sweat, and he could feel it run down into his crotch and drip off his penis. His body water ran out of his hair and into his eyes in burning, salty streams.

In a quarter of an hour his throat was parched.

After a full hour he fainted.

His bare skin was scraped raw as he collapsed in the narrow interior. Unable to fall completely, he simply slumped down until consciousness returned.

Time meant nothing by late afternoon. Felipe was so desperate for a drink that he cupped his hands and tried to urinate into them. But he was so dehydrated that the best he could do was a couple of weak, yellow drops. Nevertheless, he was grateful and licked the piss from his fingers.

After that he tried not to think of being thirsty. Felipe did his best to force his mind to remember pleasant things in the past. But his thoughts always returned to water—clear, cold, refreshing water. The next few hours dissolved into bouts of unconsciousness, jumbled thoughts and a driving, instinctive need to quench his thirst.

Then, without warning, the door was jerked open, and Felipe fell out of the box to the ground. Hands gripped him under the arms and dragged him across the dirt to the guardhouse a few meters away.

Even though the temperature outside was 120 degrees, it seemed to the prisoner as if an air conditioner had been turned on. He greedily sucked the cooler air past his parched lips. When he was thrown inside the shade of the small building, he thought he was in paradise. The cement floor felt as if it was made of ice.

Sergeant Zotol sat on a table in the middle of the room. "How do you like our accommodations on this side of the prison?"

"Very warm," Felipe replied. He had learned how to answer questions from the guards by then.

Zotol displayed his version of a smile. "I'll bet you'd like a nice drink of cold water, then to be taken back to your barracks to spend the rest of the day recuperating from your time in the hot box, eh?"

Felipe nodded. *"Sí, mi sargento."*

"Then all you have to do is tell me how you helped that miserable bastard to escape," Zotol said.

Felipe was weak now, but not to the point of stupidity. "I didn't help him."

"Then you know who did, right?"

Felipe shook his head. "I didn't even know he had escaped, *mi sargento*."

Zotol said nothing for a full two minutes. Then he stood up with a nod of his head.

Two soldiers, unnoticed by Felipe as they stood behind him by the door, stepped up and grabbed him hard, throwing him down on the table on which Zotol had been sitting. They secured the prisoner on the crude piece of furniture with several leather restraining straps. Then they stepped back.

Zotol leaned over Felipe. "Now, I ask you again. When and how did you help the prisoner escape?"

Felipe licked his dry lips. "I didn't help him."

"Who did?"

"I don't know anything about the escape," Felipe insisted weakly.

Zotol barked a quick order. *"¡El teléfono!"*

Felipe grimaced in pain as two pinching objects were hooked onto the loose skin of his scrotum.

Zotol's face appeared again. "You are now attached to a field telephone. Do you know what that means?"

Felipe's dry eyes were unable to produce tears despite the biting pain. "No, *mi sargento*."

"I'll just give it a little crank."

A sharp stab of pain hit Felipe. He involuntarily jerked violently.

"Now, I ask you the question again," Zotol said. "What did you do to help the escape succeed?"

"I don't know anything about the escape," Felipe said hoarsely.

The agony slammed into him with the wave of electrical charge. Felipe's back arched as he strained against his bonds. He screamed loudly, his croaking voice rising to a screech of despair and suffering.

Then it stopped.

"We are just starting," Zotol said.

Felipe rolled his eyes heavenward. *"Dios, dejame morir por favor*—please, God, let me die!"

The crank on the telephone spun again, and Felipe prayed that he would be called.

11

The launch rocked crazily as several rounds hit it. Track, his voice almost drowned out by the fusillade of both incoming and outgoing rounds, pointed to the bank on the left. "Head that way!"

Laredo, on the tiller, instantly obeyed. Hessler grabbed his henchman's carbine and clumsily worked the cocking handle of the Winchester. He fired off an ineffective round while at the same time bellowing in rage, "No! No! Go to the opposite side! This is where the ambushers are!"

But by then the boat, with the other beside it, had hit the soft bank. Track instantly leaped over the box, and rushed into the vegetation, running into its protective cover for five meters before stopping. He was immediately joined by Zulu and George.

Then Hessler made an appearance with both Laredo and Rafael behind him. The little man was furious. "Are you stupid, Track! We should have gone through that ambush!"

"You're the stupid shit around here," Track said calmly. He checked his weapon as he spoke. "Those boats move too slow to break through fields of fire like those we were facing."

Hessler sputtered and waved his arms. "Then why come on this side where the bandits are? There's more safety on the other bank."

Track spoke matter-of-factly. "I'm not looking for safety, Hessler. I'm gonna kick some ass. That's the best way to deal with this situation. We have to come back this way. That means if we sneak through on the other side, these bastards will be waiting for our return trip."

Hessler calmed down. "Ah, yes. I see."

Zulu cranked the charging handle on the Uzi. "They won't be able to interfere with us again if they're dead."

Hessler wasn't cowed, but he was impressed. He spoke with a new respect in his voice. "My men and I will do what you wish."

Track pointed to Hessler's holster where the snub-nosed .38 was nestled. "That piece you're packing is damned near useless, but it could be effective for close jungle fighting. Provided you get it out and use it."

"If you insist," Hessler said. He produced the weapon, but the way he held it indicated that he would only use it if absolutely necessary. Don Juan Hessler was not the type of man to show any overt aggressive tendencies.

"In the meantime," Track said, motioning toward the sound of the firing that had now dropped off to sporadic individual shots, "let's go kill some people."

Track and Company were an experienced, well-rehearsed team. They formed into a three-man fire unit and moved toward the sound of the firing.

Track made the first contact.

A bandit, shirtless but wearing a pair of oversize trousers he had stolen in a raid, aimed a .30-06 sporting rifle toward the river. His head was tipped back slightly as he searched the watery area in front of him for somebody to shoot. The bullets he had were few and expensive.

Track brought up the SPAS-12 and squeezed off a round of buckshot. The blast, roaring across a bare four meters of space, shredded meat from the bandit's body to expose bare ribs and pink lungs in one splattering millisecond, while at the same instant, the man was hurled through the natural cover and landed in the river.

The piranha made an instant appearance.

Several meters to the side of Track and a bit farther forward, Zulu sniffed, his nostrils working efficiently until he was sure in which direction the unwashed bodies were located. He swung the muzzle of the Uzi that way and pumped off several quick firebursts.

Screams of agony and rage immediately followed. There was the sound of somebody clumsily—and painfully—staggering through the brush toward the river. After a brief pause, there was a splash. Horrible screams then erupted as the meat-eating fish attacked living flesh.

George Beegh, slightly deafened by both the blast from Track's shotgun and the fusillade from Zulu's submachine gun, moved slowly forward, distracted by the buzzing in his ear. Unable to hear clearly, he relied totally on his sight as he eased through the thick entanglement of jungle brush.

Suddenly the bark of a tree beside his head exploded and a geyser of earth erupted at his feet. Confused, he fired to the front, but another round whipped past his face—downward.

George—his mind and reflexes guiding his body in instantaneous, instinctive commands—flopped over onto his back. Pointing the 9-millimeter AR-15 upward, he cut loose with a half-dozen shots.

The sniper in the tree took one round through a foot hanging over a limb, and two more in his buttocks. A fourth bullet punched in under his chin, bounced off facial bones, then exited through the rear of his skull.

George rolled over to avoid the body as it toppled out of the tree and slammed to the soft jungle earth.

Don Juan Hessler had taken up a rearward position, making sure that both Laredo and Rafael were in front of him. They had no targets of opportunity, blocked by the fire team ahead of them, and they stumbled over the dead bodies of the three unlucky bandits.

Rafael, anxious to use the Mauser M-88 rifle he'd brought with him, looked over at Laredo. "Those three *hombres* are good, *compañero*."

Laredo, cradling his 30-30, nodded in agreement. "Yes. You should have seen them in that firefight in front of the hotel."

"We saved them!" Hessler said. "If you and those other two *tipos* hadn't been there, they'd be dead meat at this moment."

"I don't think so," Laredo said. "Anybody else would've gone down long before, but they were still alive and fighting. I bet those three would have made it to safety inside the hotel, eh?"

"Never!" Hessler said. "Wait a moment. I want to talk to you." The three of them stopped and pulled back several meters to the rear. Hessler glanced around to make sure that no one was near. When he spoke again, it was in a whisper. "Those three are *idiotas*, got it? We are duping them and everybody else about that calendar."

Laredo shrugged. "I figured that. I know you well, Hessler. No doubt you lied to us about the true value of the thing we're after, so I'm willing to work hard for my share. But I want a foolproof plan before I pull any *mierda* on those fellows. Especially that Track. He's tough—a real dangerous type."

Hessler tapped his head. "Brains always overcome brawn and blustering. Track is a headstrong dunce who is playing into my hands."

Laredo wasn't convinced, but he didn't want to pick any arguments with Hessler at that point. "*Bien*, you're the boss, Hessler."

"And don't you forget it—ever!" Hessler snarled. He turned and glared at Rafael.

Rafael shrugged. "Hey. I'm not arguing, am I?"

"See that you don't," Hessler warned him.

"I don't see why you brought them along, though," Rafael complained.

"I didn't want to," Hessler explained. "But the people who insured this expedition insisted on it." Then he laughed softly. "For their sake, I hope they're not carrying any life insurance policies on Track and his two companions."

Rafael grinned.

Laredo was more practical. "It turns out they're a blessing to us. If it wasn't for those three, we'd be pinned down in this stinking jungle by those *chingando* bandits."

Hessler's temper erupted. "Track and his friends are not supermen! Why do you insist on giving them more credit than they are due?"

Laredo started to protest. "I'm not—"

A sudden outbreak of shots crashed through the heavy, hot air. Hessler's head snapped in that direction. "Somebody up there is dying. Perhaps our problem with the bandits and with Track is being solved at this moment."

COLONEL JORGE TORRES STOOD on the small platform that had been set out in the middle of the Camp Oro yard. He was dressed in his tailored camouflage fatigue uniform, complete with red beret and spit-shined jump boots. The accessories he wore were also of polished leather and consisted of a heavy belt, holster, magazine holder and shoulder harness.

He was the perfect picture of the stern, brave, military commander.

The poor wretches formed up in front of him were clad in shorts and huarache sandals. They were so closely packed together that their shaved heads looked like a collection of melons. Soldiers, their red headgear bobbing about in agitated movements, circulated among the convicts, making sure that strict order and silence were observed.

Finally, his voice loud and booming, Colonel Torres spoke.

"A great crime has been committed against the Peruvian people," he began. "It saddens me greatly to report to you that an evil man among you has turned his back on the mercy of our republic's government and rejected our benevolent philosophy of freedom through hard work." Torres's voice rose to a great intensity, the rage in it cowing the assembled prisoners. "He has escaped! Escaped! ESCAPED!"

A good many of the men in the ranks glanced fearfully at the soldiers who surrounded them. They expected a steel-jacketed hail of machine-gun bullets to slam into the crowd at any moment.

But Torres's voice returned to normal. "To compound this heinous misdeed, the individual who ran away enlisted others to help him. His squad mates assisted in his escape. But I am sure you will be pleased to know that we have gotten the truth of the matter from them." He paused to raise a cautioning finger. "You all—every man—must keep in mind that if one member of your squad runs away, you will all—*todos*—be held responsible. That is the law—my law—and my justice is swift and sure." He turned toward Sergeant Zotol. "Bring the culprits forward!"

Zotol marched the short distance to the guardhouse and stepped inside. Moments later he emerged leading a pathetic line of six men toward the platform. The half-dozen convicts shuffled slowly and painfully up to the platform. They were turned to face the crowd.

The convicts, used to seeing cruelty dealt to their kind, had never seen anything this bad. All six were naked. Raw wounds and bruises covered their bodies. Their genitals, electrified countless times, were swollen and burned.

"There were nine of them," Torres said in a calm voice. "But God in his terrible wrath claimed the three most culpable. They died under questioning. The remaining six have now received my official sentence. They are to receive *el Trato*. That means they will work eighteen hours a day on a regimen of five hundred calories of food—until God calls them to His own form of justice."

Felipe Rodriguez, one of the miserable survivors, now knew his fate. He couldn't visualize five hundred calories of food, but he knew it wouldn't be much. It all added up to his being worked and starved to death. A quick death from a soldier's submachine gun would be better, but the young prisoner knew that any defiance on his part would only prolong the inevitable—with an interim of electrical torture to make things worse. He looked at the other convicts through his swollen eyes. If he'd been able, he would have formed his battered mouth into a smile.

Now, deep in his heart, Felipe felt he was one of the fortunate ones in Camp Oro—he would be leaving soon.

TRACK, THE SPAS-12 LOADED with its usual alternating rounds of solid slug and buckshot, squatted in the thicket. He could hear the babbling of the bandits around him, and he knew the undisciplined rabble were having a morale problem. Not only had their impromptu ambush with its promise of loot gone to hell for them, but their limited numbers were rapidly diminished.

At that moment, a half dozen of their fellows had gone to that great lair in the sky, and three of them were already being digested by the insatiable piranhas. The fish, even though they were close to being gorged, were still in a feeding frenzy, snapping at the empty water.

Track had taken a chance in giving away his hiding place with a bellowed order at Zulu and George to stand fast. But, in the thick vegetation, it had been necessary. With visibility in some places at less than two meters, it would have been disastrously easy for them to have shot each other during any uncoordinated hunting.

The bandits had been chattering like magpies among themselves for the previous ten minutes. Track didn't need to know Spanish to understand what was going on. Anger, defiance and frustration come through a man's voice no matter what language he bitches in.

And bitching also gives away his position.

Track now knew where he wanted to go. He belly-crawled in a slow, deliberate fashion for less than ten meters and then he peered ahead at ground level until he could identify four sets of feet.

The long minutes of listening had convinced him that these were the last of the gang.

Track stood up, changing from a gradual motion into a lightning-fast spasm of pure speed.

He leaped into the clearing, the SPAS-12 muzzle at waist level. The first shot—a solid slug—hit Bandit Survivor One in the chest with a slightly upward trajectory. The man was lifted off his feet and slammed into a mahogany tree behind him.

Round number two, buckshot, blew Survivor Two—a skinny fellow—into two hunks of ex-bandit.

Survivor Three literally lost his head to the heavy solid slug that crashed into his jaw. The final round hit Survivor

Four in the buttocks as the man—who had a bit more time than his buddies—made an attempt to escape the specter of death that had suddenly materialized before his eyes. Poised in shock, he quickly bled to death as the large arteries in his upper thighs hosed the ground with his life's blood.

Then Track, never a man to take unnecessary chances, pumped more rounds into the surrounding brush in case there was anyone he might have missed.

This is called Equal Opportunity Killing.

Silence greeted the effort. "All clear," Track yelled.

Moments later his companions joined him. Zulu, always the master of understatement, made a quick survey. "I believe I may say, without fear of contradiction, that this portion of our journey is terminated."

Hessler wasted no time. "Then I think it imperative that we return to the boats." He waited until Track and Company had preceded him. Then he motioned to Laredo and Rafael to follow.

Laredo counted the bodies of the dead bandits as they returned to the river. He whistled low. "In less than a half hour, the entire fighting force of a bandit village has been destroyed."

"Seguro," Rafael echoed. "And almost single-handed by Señor Track."

Hessler's temper soared. He whipped around and glared at his men. "I didn't say killing Track would be easy, did I?" He breathed heavily through clenched teeth. "But you will see it can be done."

Rafael was a brave man. "Of course. Dan Track won't be the first fellow that I have both admired and destroyed."

"Now you know why I chose you for this job," Hessler said. He pointed to Laredo. "You too."

Laredo grinned. He liked a challenge.

12

Night had closed in on Camp Oro, and the compound was quiet as exhausted men slept. The only noise around them was the quiet tread of sentries' boots and the hissing of gasoline lanterns that cast a dim light in the prison yard.

Outside the confines of the man-made hell, there was another kind of Hades—a natural one. The jungle was permeated with an inky blackness in which night killers prowled in search of food. Daytime creatures—and the prey of the nocturnal hunters—had established their individual sanctuaries during the late-evening hours when there had been light to find burrows or build quick nests in the safety of treetops. Each species of animal and insect followed its instincts, and the night echoed eerily with their cries and screeches.

But none of these sounds reached the interior of Colonel Jorge Torres's quarters. The hum of the air conditioner drowned out the jungle noises, as did the tinkling of the ice in the drinks that he and Sergeant Emiliano Zotol enjoyed with the two women visiting them.

The females were no beauties—a pretty woman was hard to find in this godforsaken wilderness—but they were young and had passably attractive bodies. Both were Indians who had been semicivilized by contact with whites in Rio Vista. As third-generation residents of the town, they had adopted the Spanish language, western clothing and harlotry as ways to make good lives for themselves. Their destinies, unfortunately, were miserable. Venereal disease and alcoholism would lay them out before they reached the age of forty. This was the curse of many South American Indians who succumbed to civilization.

Two or three times a month a soldier in a jeep called for the two women at the bordello where they were regularly employed. After they dressed properly, they were taken out to Camp Oro.

At this point in the early evening, as always, they were ignored by the two paratroopers, who spent the time discussing business. The two whores availed themselves generously of Colonel Torres's bar. Being intoxicated helped them bear what usually happened during these sporadic episodes at the prison camp.

The colonel was completely relaxed. He'd taken off his fatigue jacket and jump boots. Attired in trousers, T-shirt and thick army socks, he stretched out comfortably in the recliner he'd bought at the PX at Fort Gulick in Panama during his last visit there. He raised his glass containing Dewar's and club soda. *"A la Batallón de Paracaidistas-Casadores,"* he toasted. "To the Parachutist Commando Battalion."

Across from him, Sergeant Emiliano Zotol raised his can of beer. *"¡A la batallón!"* he echoed. The NCO had relaxed by unbuttoning his jacket. He was seated on a large leather sofa that completely dominated one side of the living room. An ashtray, containing his slowly burning cigar, sat by his elbow. He drained the can in a few large swallows. Immediately one of the Indian women scurried over with another full one. She bent over far enough to allow him a long leer down the front of her dress. Zotol appreciated her beauty, but he gave the whore no compliments. Instead he turned his eyes back to his commandant. "We are short of men."

Torres nodded. "I agree. Perhaps my idea of making that squad an example for the escape was not such a good idea."

"It is always a good idea to administer mass punishment. That encourages the prisoners to keep an eye on each other and inform on malcontents and troublemakers. So, under normal circumstances, your idea would have been an excellent one," Zotol said respectfully.

"Yes, but we hardly have a situation around here that could be called normal," Torres said. He rubbed his hand across his close-cropped, balding pate. "And I wanted to increase the production of gold."

Zotol's slits of eyes widened a bit. "Is there anything special coming up, *mi coronel*?"

"Possibly," Torres answered. "I have finally reached a point where I can make some contacts with some other army units—and some naval ones too."

"The New Empire could certainly use a ship," Zotol commented.

"Not to mention a plane or two, eh, Sergeant?" Torres laughed. "Or should I say 'Colonel'?"

"Then I should address you as 'Marshal,'" Zotol said.

"Let us wait until the time is right," Torres said. "I feel it is bad luck to become cocksure."

"Of course, *mi coronel*," Zotol said. He raised his can of beer. "But allow me to say, '*Hoy Peru, Mañana el Mundo*—Today Peru, Tomorrow the World.'"

"I will always drink to that. The blood of two great peoples is intermingled in our veins—the great Incan empire builders and the grand conquerors from Spain. It is our destiny to be great rulers," Torres said. He finished his Scotch and then set the empty glass down and pointed to it. The other woman, swinging her hips provocatively, sauntered over with a fresh one. She did not have to hurry with the colonel as her friend did with the sergeant. Her officer had more taste and liked to take his pleasure at a leisurely pace.

Torres's eyes ate her up while, at the same time, he continued his conversation with Zotol. "I forgot to tell you that the arms purchases in Bolivia went quite well."

"Were they curious about the gold?" Zotol asked.

"Of course," Torres said. "Most weapons transactions are with American dollars. I explained the gold came from drug deals via Colombia. I figured that the more names and places bandied about, the more confusion."

"Yes, Colonel," Zotol said. "But actually the supplier doesn't really give a damn."

"Mmm," Torres agreed with a nod. "But if he's ever arrested and questioned, he'll be a confusing subject for any interrogator as he blabs out garbage that can never be followed up. At this particular time it would be most awkward if the authorities in the capital found out about our private prison and what we are doing here."

"Don't worry, *mi coronel*," Zotol assured him. "You have a hundred percent loyalty from every trooper in the battalion."

The woman returned with Torres's drink. He took it and smiled at her, then slipped his hand under the hem of her skirt. Slowly Torres caressed the whore's leg as he worked upward. She wore no underwear per instructions, and feigned pleasure as his fingers finally reached her crotch and probed at her.

Zotol waited until his commanding officer had finished amusing himself before he spoke again. "We will need armor for the taking of Lima."

"I have already thought of that," Torres said. "I have made preliminary arrangements for some British vehicles—

FV21 Foxes to be exact. I realize they are only armored cars, but they will work fine until some actual tanks become available through armor units.''

Zotol was given another beer as he spoke. ''It is imperative that we bring at least one complete tank brigade over to our side.''

''That is why I must depend on you so much,'' Torres said. ''Without the noncommissioned officer cadre backing us up all the way, we will fail miserably.''

''Do not worry,'' Zotol informed him.

''But I do worry,'' Torres said seriously. ''There are approximately sixty-five thousand men in the Peruvian army and another twenty thousand in the Guardia Civil. The bulk of them, naturally, are enlisted men. They are more loyal to their *sargentos* than to their *capitánes* and *coroneles*.''

''The sergeants—and myself in particular—will not fail the New Empire, *mi coronel*,'' Zotol assured him. ''We have been looking for a strong leader to finally set Peru on a proper course.''

''Much power can be gained through gold,'' Torres said. Then he rephrased his statement. ''All power can be gained through gold. Once South America belongs to the New Empire, we shall move north. After the hemisphere is ours, then we turn toward the rest of the world.''

Zotol again lifted his can of beer. *''¡Hoy Peru, Mañana el Mundo!''*

COLONEL Jorge Tomas Antonio Torres-Fernandez entered the world as the heir apparent of a wealthy Trujillo banking family.

As a growing boy he was pampered, overfed, spoiled and indulged. Tall for his age, Jorge was also exceedingly fat, making him appear much older than his actual years. School photos showed him towering over his classmates, looking like a glowering Latin American Buddha. Even schoolteachers let Jorge get away with things that would have brought the rod down hard on the bottom of any other errant student. His family's power and prestige, in a corrupt society in which only the barest of democratic principles are followed, stayed the hand of many an irate educator.

When Jorge reached puberty he was certainly nothing much to look at. His face, dominated by fat cheeks and pug nose, seemed frozen in a permanent frown even though he enjoyed a life-style that allowed him to do pretty much as he pleased. Like the boy whose father owned the candy store, Jorge had reached the zenith of his existence. There was nothing to dream about, or work toward or enjoy anymore. By the age of sixteen he was pretty much burned out.

Then he discovered sex.

In Latin American society, a boy becomes a man when he has fulfilled three requirements: taken a woman, fought a bull and planted a tree. The latter two were beyond Jorge's abilities or interests. He was too fat and slow to fight a bull, and too damned lazy to dig a hole in which to drop a seed. But taking a woman was within his abilities.

So the father, following normal custom, took his son to the nearest whorehouse when the lad reached the age of eighteen. The boy was scared witless when he went upstairs with the prostitute. But she was experienced in dealing with the first-timers. She was courteous and considerate, showing a great deal of sympathy and a willingness to help him along. Finally, after using all her skills and womanliness to get him up for it, the job was done and Jorge walked downstairs with a silly grin on his face.

A sexual Frankenstein's monster had been created that night.

The Torres family's upstairs maid was a young woman from the country. She had seen Jorge many times before, of course, but the boy had scarcely looked at her. Things were different now.

One Sunday evening, after Jorge had come home from visiting his grandparents, he happened to catch the girl upstairs alone. The same desires he had experienced in whorehouses welled up in him. He went for the maid in a direct, unabashed way.

The seduction, though crude, was effective.

The unfortunate girl was the first of three domestics who became pregnant through Jorge's activities. His mother was distraught, his two younger brothers amused and his father outraged.

By then Jorge was nineteen. He showed absolutely no potential, and it was obvious that he would be a one-man disaster in the family bank. Therefore, like all useless sons of the wealthy, he was packed off into the army with a purchased commission.

His sojourn into soldiering was really only an extension of his normal life—except he wore a uniform. He was assigned to an infantry brigade that, like all others, was run by the sergeants while the officers enjoyed their private incomes with plenty of revelry, drinking and wenching. Jorge grew softer and fatter, and his young face began to show hints of the ravages of heavy drinking. Then something unusual happened. Second Lieutenant Jorge Torres received orders for some real training.

He was packed off to the United States Army's School of the Americas in the Panama Canal Zone. There, for the first time, he received extensive military training. He also saw firsthand some damned good units. The American infantry stationed there were experts in jungle warfare. Tough and disciplined, they went about their duties in a highly efficient manner. There were paratroopers, Green Berets, rangers and recon marines popping up all over the place. Jorge was fascinated.

These elite troopers touched something deep inside his Hispanic macho psyche. He wanted to be like them, so he volunteered for extra training outside the classroom. He took hard physical training, jungle and guerrilla warfare courses, and even attended the parachute school run by the Panamanian National Guard.

Torres returned to Peru slim, trim, hard and mean—a paratrooper. He didn't want any more garrison bullshit; he wanted to get out into bandit country with the paratrooper-commandos and kick some ass.

The Peruvian army was only too glad to oblige him.

Ten years later, Torres was a full colonel in command of one of the best paratroop-commando battalions in the service. It seemed he would be content with the role for the rest of his life when a patrol he was leading through the jungle came across a crazed old prospector.

The man had bags of gold nuggets. The sight of these riches brought out another side of Torres—greed. Through a combination of friendly questions and tough interrogation, Torres discovered the man had come across an ancient Incan gold mine and was digging his fortune out of it.

A quick bullet in the back of the head in the dense jungle ended any legal squabbles over ownership. Torres claimed the mine for himself and set about finding a way to work it in a big way. His closest confidant was not one of his officers. Rather it was a sergeant named Zotol. This situation was not unusual in Latin American armies. Officers were constantly conniving and scheming against each other, while their sergeants showed doglike loyalty and obedience to them. Torres, with Zotol's aid and counsel, began operating the mine using prisoners taken in combat against bandits. They set up a special company of trusted troopers to help them, while the bulk of the battalion was transferred to a far side of their military department.

The scheme grew and expanded as more prisoners were taken. Wandering Indians, prospectors, hunters or anyone else unlucky enough to be policed up by Torres's troopers received a bogus court martial trial. The sentence was always the same: hard labor at Camp Oro, supposedly the official prison work camp of the republic.

As his wealth increased, so did Torres's ambitions. From dreaming of simply becoming rich, he progressed through fantasies of power. At first he envisioned himself as absolute master of the jungle province where he was stationed. But after a while that wasn't enough. He decided to control the entire nation, until the final glorious fantasy of *Imperio Nuevo*—the New Empire—occurred to him. Thus, as the size of his gold hoard grew beyond his wildest dreams, he formed the wild plan to rule the world.

After all, money was everything. With it, a man could buy arms, men, even entire nations to work for him. To Colonel Jorge Torres, it was all quite logical and plausible. All he had to do was get enough gold—and that could be done by maintaining a slave population to work the mine.

And that meant that any man entering the uninhabited jungles of his territory would end up serving a life sentence in this new, diabolical order.

TORRES TOOK THE FRESH DRINK. "My real woman will be here soon," he said. He winked at the whore. "Not that you're not a real pleasure, my dove. But a man like myself craves beauty and class in the women he beds."

"What day will she arrive?" Zotol asked.

"I expect a letter," Torres answered. "When I know, I'll dispatch a couple of men in a jeep to Rio Vista to pick her up." He stood up and nodded at the prostitute while motioning toward his bedroom. "In the meantime, I shall get what pleasure I can, when I can."

Zotol displayed his lopsided grin. "Me too, *mi coronel*." He got up and walked across the room to grab the other woman.

She allowed herself to be taken out of the house over to Zotol's quarters. She knew that, before morning, every orifice of her body would be violated.

13

The man stood on a narrow, grassy slope that spread down from the jungle to the river. He gave no indication that he saw the two boats other than to keep his eyes riveted to the lead launch.

Hessler stood up. "Hello, Correro." He motioned to Laredo. "Go to shore here."

The boats turned in, running gently into the bank. The man called Correro merely watched as the craft were hauled ashore. He continued his silence as they were hidden inside the tree line. Finally, when the six men who had just arrived stood ready with rucksacks and weapons in hand, Correro pointed into the jungle.

"Por alla," he said, and strolled off into the rain forest.

Track, with Hessler hot on his heels, followed Correro down a narrow trail that had only recently been hacked out with the jungle man's machete. After a brief five-minute walk the group emerged into a small clearing.

This was Correro's camp. It consisted of an open fireplace for cooking that was bordered on three sides with short logs put there as seats. Off to one side, he had built a lean-to made of palm fronds laid on a frame of tree limbs. A large mosquito net had been thrown over the affair to complete its construction.

Correro sat down by the smoldering fire. He was a thin man, with thick dark brows over dark eyes that darted constantly around as if perpetually on the lookout for potential enemies. He was dressed in nondescript Levi's and a cotton shirt.

Hessler remained standing but everyone else sat down. He pointed to Track. "This is the man appointed to oversee this transaction. His name is Track."

Track nodded, using some of the Spanish he had been acquiring. *"Mucho gusto."*

"Igualmente," Correro replied.

Hessler felt the need to offer some further explanation. "Correro is a professional poacher," he explained. "And when he isn't running the jungle himself, he acts as an agent for others of his kind."

George Beegh, a gun enthusiast, was not favorably impressed. He glared at the man. "What do you deal in? Leopard skins and caiman hides along with the remains of other endangered species?"

"Of course," Correro replied matter-of-factly. "How else would there be a profit in poaching?"

George frowned. "Guys like you give honest hunters a bad name."

Track was more pragmatic. "He doesn't give a shit, George." He motioned to Hessler. "Let's get this deal consummated, huh?"

Hessler looked at Correro. *"Ensenale el calendario de Pizarro."*

Correro stood up and walked around the lean-to into the jungle. He returned a few moments later lugging an object wrapped in a tarpaulin. He set it down in front of Track. *"Miralo si quiere."*

"He said to look at it if you wish," Hessler explained.

Track pulled the weighty object upright. "It's heavy all right," he acknowledged. He undid the greasy rope holding the tarp in place. When it fell away, there was a round object taped up tightly in tar paper. Track peeled this away. What he saw made him whistle aloud. "Jesus!"

"Wow!" George said.

Zulu's eyes widened. *"C'est magnifique!* Pardon my French."

The calendar was indeed magnificent. Highlighted against the gold, its jewels sparkled in the sunlight that filtered through the tall jungle trees. Hieroglyphics and other designs of the ancient Incan empire adorned the beautiful work of art.

Unknown to the modern men in that jungle clearing, this same object had been wrested from the dying hands of a greedy, young hidalgo more than four centuries previously.

"Gentlemen, you are looking at history," Zulu said.

Hessler didn't give a damn about historical value or aura. His mind was on the commercial side of the enterprise. "Are you satisfied, Mr. Track?"

"I'm no expert on these things," Track said. He nudged Zulu. "What do you think, my learned friend?"

"I am positive this is the genuine article," Zulu said. "As an archaeologist, I am overwhelmed."

George felt compelled to brag a bit for his companion. "Zulu holds a Ph.D. in archaeology from Oxford."

Hessler raised his eyebrows. "I am quite impressed, Mr. Zulu."

Correro lit a thick cigar. "It is genuine," he said in English. Then he looked at George Beegh. He had completely concealed his irritation with the young American, but he betrayed the feelings of resentment when he said, "If American vanity did not make it profitable to poach jungle cats and other creatures, we would not do it."

"You can also say that if American dopers didn't make smuggling profitable, then the crime rate in the western hemisphere would drop appreciably," George retorted.

"But that doesn't make me an apologist for narcotics gangsters."

"Knock it off," Track said. "We're here to buy this thing, not discuss the weaknesses of modern civilization."

"Correction, Mr. Track," Hessler said. "It is I who am here to buy Pizarro's calendar."

"Then buy it, Hessler."

Hessler pulled his rucksack from his shoulders. He opened it and reached inside, producing a large packet. He tossed it over to Correro. "It's all there."

Correro maintained his poker face. "You know I can't count, Hessler. But if you have shorted me, I will find out. And I will kill you."

Hessler's temper flared. "Don't threaten me! I won't take that, you jungle-running bastard!" He tumbled at his holster to pull the snub-nosed Smith & Wesson free. Correro leaped across the distance between them, producing a knife at the same instant. A quick slash and Hessler backed out of the way. But he dropped his pistol to the ground before Correro continued his assault.

Track, Zulu and George swung their own weapons over on Laredo and Rafael, who were about to do the same to Correro. Track's voice was cold and sharp. "Drop 'em!"

The two gunsels stopped. They sized up the SPAS-12, AR-15 and Uzi muzzles turned on them. Their weapons hit the dirt.

Hessler's famous temper calmed. He laughed nervously. "Say! What are we doing here, eh? We are all friends."

"You know, Hessler, you're about a hair away from being stark raving crazy," Track said angrily. "You damn near created a situation here that could have cost some lives."

Hessler shrugged. "I am a man of strong passions."

"You'd better start controlling those emotions around me, man," Track said. He turned to the group. "Everybody sit down and take a deep breath."

The little campsite calmed down for a few moments. It was Zulu who finally broke the silence. His enthusiasm overshadowed the danger of the situation. "Tell me, Mr. Correro. Can you acquire more historical articles such as this one?"

"I know of none at the moment," Correro answered. "But the man who supplied me with this may know—"

Hessler leaped to his feet. "Correro is *my* contact!" he yelled. "You have no right to butt in on my arrangements with him."

"Shut up, Hessler," Track said.

"I will not!" Hessler shrieked. "I'll kill you first, Track! Do you hear me!"

"Yes. I hear you," Track responded calmly. "I imagine the folks back in Rio Vista hear you, too. Let's get a couple of things straight now. I wasn't kidding when I told you to rein in that temper of yours, and most assuredly, I don't conduct the business of my clients by your rules or for your private advantage. You're getting a damned good deal out of this Pizarro's calendar. Dr. Cordoba said that if the Peruvian government got in on this, no one except some crooked politician would benefit."

Hessler sat down, sinking into a morose silence.

Correro's frown deepened. "To hell with all of you! I shall conduct my business as it suits me—and that means I deal with whom I please."

"Good enough," Track said. He didn't want to irritate an already uneasy situation. "Let's all forget about everything except getting Pizarro's calendar back to civilization."

Correro laughed and waved the packet of money. "Frankly, I don't think anyone but myself will benefit from this deal." Then he sobered, speaking almost fearfully as if some great revelation had come to him. "The *indios* way back in the jungle said that calendar had a curse on it. I believe them. This disk of gold will bring death to more than one man before it is back in Lima—if it ever gets there."

FELIPE RODRIGUEZ STRUGGLED to raise the pick over his head. When he finally did, he let the tool fall of its own accord into the earthen wall of the mine.

"Lazy bastard!" The soldier's accusing voice echoed in the small confines of the cavern where he and the other survivors of his squad worked. The trooper stepped forward and kicked Felipe in the side of the knee.

His legs went out from under him and he fell to the muddy floor. He struggled as rapidly as he could to regain his feet, and his arms trembled with the effort. He endured another kick and a hard cuff on the back of the neck before he managed to stand up. He did his best to show some enthusiasm as he resumed his struggle with the pick, but his body was growing close to the point of collapse.

He and his fellows had been enduring *el Trato*—the Treatment—for more than a week.

Forced to sleep in the mine where they worked, with no sunshine to mitigate the effects of the damp environment, the men were suffering from bouts of pain in inflamed joints. This condition was particularly bad at the start of their workday when the guards kicked them awake at four o'clock in the morning.

Within ten minutes of the rude call to duty, their picks and shovels would be digging into the dirt. With the pace kept at a high level through the enthusiastic attention of the soldiers, they were close to collapse before their only daily meal arrived at midday, eight hours after their long shift began.

Dry bread and a gourd of water had to be consumed within ten minutes, and while standing up. At no time during their eighteen-hour shift were they allowed to kneel or sit.

The original six brought into *el Trato* were now down to four. One man had simply keeled over from heart failure. Two days after he'd been dragged unceremoniously out of the mine, another had dropped his shovel. He turned toward the guard, his face a mask of despair and hopelessness. "Kill me now," he begged him, "I cannot endure more of this."

They killed him, but not quickly or particularly efficiently. After several long hours with Sergeant Zotol's telephone, the miserable convict was kicked back to the work crew and beaten to death in front of the four survivors when he was unable to respond to commands to work.

Felipe decided that death by heart failure due to exhaustion was preferable to going back to the insidious electricity that slammed so hard into a man's body it must surely rattle his soul. The young ex-bandit swung his pick as best he could, feeling that each individual effort brought him closer to that Great Releaser—Death.

HESSLER WAS AGITATED AS HELL. He knew that Track would inform Dr. Cordoba of the National Museum of the fact that future transactions could be made directly with the poacher Correro. No doubt, Cordoba and his people would prefer to bypass Hessler to reach the jungle man and deal personally for Incan objects. That would cut Hessler out of a great deal of profit. Correro's prices were ridiculously low. The man might be sharp as hell in transactions involving hides and furs, but when it came to gold or historical artifacts, he was a babe in the woods—literally.

Hessler smiled to himself. The idiot had actually taken the equivalent of a thousand American dollars for Pizarro's calendar. By keeping the real details of the trade from Track, Hessler could realize an amount of money that would set him up for years in the best apartments with beautiful women, vintage wine and all the good things a jet-setter could enjoy.

He downed the last of his coffee and stood up. The other men were lounging around Correro's camp during these final hours of daylight. "Laredo, Rafael! Come with me," Hessler said. He glared at Track. "Am I permitted to caucus with my men?"

Track shrugged. "There's not much I can do about it, is there?"

"You could murder us," Hessler suggested in a sarcastic tone.

"Don't tempt me, Hessler," Track said calmly.

"Bah!" He turned and walked into the jungle with Laredo and Rafael following. When Hessler was satisfied they were out of earshot of the camp, he stopped. "We cannot allow Track and his two friends to return to Lima."

Laredo nodded. "Of course. But you have already told us that, Hessler."

Rafael nervously licked his lips. "Do you have any particular plans?"

"I do now," Hessler said. "Do you remember the last shallows we went through, when we had to portage around them?"

"Of course," Laredo said. "That was about a half day from Correro's camp."

"That is where we shall kill Mr. Track and his pals," Hessler said. "After we leave the shallows and walk around them, I shall say there is a rock in my boot. Everyone will wait while I remove it. That is when you prepare yourselves." He pointed to Laredo. "You are to get the young hellion Beegh. And you, Rafael, may shoot the black giant." He giggled. "An easy target, no?"

Laredo didn't see any humor in the situation. "It will have to be well coordinated and simultaneous. Particularly if you are going to shoot down Track."

"I most assuredly am," Hessler promised. "I will prepare you by saying, 'The rains will come soon.' That is your cue to get ready to shoot immediately. Then, when everything is right, I will say, 'When the rains arrive, there will be much thunder.' On that last word start shooting."

Rafael was pleased. "They won't suspect a thing. You have thought this out well, Hessler."

"Of course," Hessler said. "Now let's get back to the camp. Don't alarm them by hostile words, and on the other hand don't become too friendly. That will put them on their guard, too."

"Don't worry," Rafael assured him. "By tomorrow afternoon, Track and his friends will be only a memory to us."

"And to everyone else who ever knew them," Hessler said.

14

George Beegh was definitely not enjoying himself. After a hard half-day's travel from Correro's camp back toward civilization, the weather was hot and muggy, his insect repellent was not working, he was tired, and now the water in the Riachuelo Verde was so low they had to get out and carry the launches around the shallows to deeper water on the other side.

This had been difficult enough before. But now, besides the useless surveying tools in the crate they'd had to bring along, Pizarro's calendar—all 150 pounds of it—was nestled snugly in the compartment. That meant the struggle of toting boats and equipment through the tangle of jungle around the river was much more of a chore.

Hessler was so lazy that he was useless during the hard work. When a launch was lifted, the little man would scoot under it and feign helping to hold it up while the two men on the end labored with the burden. Then, as always, he complained of some minor injury such as a twisted ankle or strained wrist. The injury necessitated his immediately resting, while the other five men went about the task of wrestling the loads into place.

Track and Laredo heaved launch number one up over their heads, then followed Zulu as he hacked a trail of sorts through the rain forest until they were past the shallow water. Although they'd come through that exact area in the same manner on the way in, the trail they had cut was already overgrown with the persistent vegetation for which the Amazonian jungle was so famous.

While they were gone, George sat on the crate keeping a sharp eye on both Hessler and Rafael. "What are you going to do with all your money, Hessler?" George asked.

"Live a good life, of course," Hessler answered. "What about you?"

George shook his head. "Dan, Zulu and I aren't getting squat from this deal. We're on retainers."

"Surely you'll get a bonus," Hessler suggested.

"No one has mentioned any," George replied.

"Yet you're all totally dedicated to completing the job," Hessler said. "Three little Boy Scouts, that's you fellows."

George started to make a wise-ass remark back, but Track, Zulu and Laredo reappeared. Track, wringing wet with sweat, wiped at his brow. "Let's get the crate next. It'll take four guys—one on each corner."

"Damn," George said. "With that frigging calendar in there, it must weigh two hundred and fifty to three hundred pounds."

"Well, it ain't going to get any lighter by just looking at it," Track said. "Let's grab it and go. Hessler?"

Hessler rubbed his knee. "I must have banged it getting out of the launch."

Track laughed. "You lazy bastard."

Hessler growled. "I'm glad you find my injury so amusing, Track."

Track was feeling mean in the heat. "Oh, fuck you!" He motioned to the others. "George, that corner. Zulu there, please. Rafael, get off your ass and take hold, too. I'll grab on right here."

The four men heaved and managed to wrest the heavy crate off the ground. They staggered through the newly reopened trail and disappeared into the trees.

Hessler yawned, glancing at Laredo. "There is one more set of shallows between here and Rio Vista. Do you think you and Rafael can handle that crate?"

"It wouldn't hurt you to help us," Laredo said with a complaining tone in his voice.

"Hey! I'm the *jefe*—the boss. I don't do the work the laborers are supposed to do. I'm the brains—you two the brawn, got it?"

"Let's wait to knock off Track and his friends after we round the second shallows," Laredo said.

"I can't let your laziness interfere with the project," Hessler said smugly.

Five minutes later Track and Zulu reappeared. "George and Rafael are with the crate," Track said. "Let's get this launch and we'll be able to sail on down to the next shallows."

Zulu tested his memory. "We shouldn't run into them until day after tomorrow."

Hessler watched as Track, Zulu and Laredo heaved the boat over their heads. He followed them down the trail to where the deeper water began. The second launch was set down and shoved into the water beside the first. Without a word everyone, with the exception of Hessler, turned to the crate and hefted it aboard the first craft.

"Shall we hop aboard and continue?" Zulu asked.

"Just a moment, please," Hessler said. "I seem to have a rock in my boot." He sat down and undid the lacing. He turned the footgear upside down, and shrugged. "Must've been something else." He slipped it back on. "The rains will come soon," he said to attract Laredo's and Rafael's attention.

Both tightened their grips on their weapons.

Hessler laced the boot back up. He leaned forward slightly as if he were about to get up, his hand swinging down to his holster. "When the rains arrive," he said, "there will be much—thunder!"

The gunfire erupted in the clearing, the concussion of whipping bullets knocking leaves from some branches.

FELIPE PULLED AT THE PICK, but he was too weak to grasp the handle. It slipped and fell to the dirt. He bent down, weary and dizzy, grabbing it again. He tried hard, but could not get the tool high enough, and it pulled him to the floor of the mine as it dropped. He hunched his shoulders, waiting for the blow he knew would come from the guard's submachine gun stock. But instead he heard a different command.

"Outside—you three—outside!"

Another of the crew had given up the ghost under the severe conditions of *el Trato*. The trio left looked incredulously at the guard.

"Didn't you scum hear me? I said for you to get out of here! Now move—*muevense pronto*!"

Felipe felt a great sense of relief and contentment. No doubt, their usefulness was finally over. Weakened to the point of near collapse, they had not done any effective work for the previous two shifts. There would be a flurry of punches and kicks, then the merciful quickness of a firing squad. He wondered what heaven would be like. Surely, as a good Christian bandit, he would go there. His father had preceded him. The old man had been shot by police nearly fifteen years previously.

And he would see Flaco, too. He would tell his cousin how lucky he had been to have been killed during that first encounter with the soldiers. Flaco had avoided a lot of physical suffering that way.

The three men emerged from the mine to find it a bit past midday. The entire convict labor force was drawn up in formation. Felipe thought it was to see the executions, but then he saw a dead body lying in front of the platform where *el coronel* Torres stood.

The three men undergoing *el Trato* were taken up to the spot. Felipe glanced down at the cadaver. He instantly recognized the cause of death—snakebite. The swollen, blackened condition of the body was one he was familiar with. He'd known of several people who had been fatally bitten in the jungle around his home village.

Colonel Torres waited until the three survivors had been pushed into a proper position before him. Then he spoke to the assembled prisoners.

"Justice is served. The escapee has been returned to us. A patrol of my soldiers found this carrion in the jungle not far from the camp. Even the devil was against this wretch. The bite of a loathsome reptile, an instrument of the devil who seduced Eve into sin, has righted the wrong committed. Of the nine men who were connected with this escape, only this trio survives. That is a great lesson for all of you. And these three were repentant throughout *el Trato*. They worked hard to show how sorry they were to have broken the laws of the republic. So, to show her mercy and reward their faithful labors, La República de Peru now pardons these prisoners and allows them to return to regular duties. They will even be given a period of rest for three days before going back to their regular work shifts. With relaxation, good food and a chance to mend their ways, they will work even harder to earn their freedom. Remember, prisoners, *Se gana libertad por trabajo*—Freedom is gained through work."

Felipe and his two companions were taken to the food issue point. Each was allowed to sip a gourd of cold water. Then they were given a bit of fish and some fruit. Even the ignorant soldiers knew that too much food at this point would kill them.

Twenty minutes later, his stomach now working at absorbing the protein and vitamins just put into it, Felipe was taken to his old barracks.

He lay down on the sleeping mat, staring up at the ceiling. He had learned something during *el Trato*. He was strong and no coward. If he could survive that ordeal, he was ready for anything else they might throw at him. Despite his physical condition, Felipe felt he'd come out of that mine a stronger, better man than he'd ever been.

He was a fighter!

Now was the time to think of getting out of here. He remembered what the Mexican fellow, Antonio Poreso, had said of a savior—a mortal messiah—coming in to lead them all to freedom. Felipe decided he would eat well to let his strength return. He wanted to be ready for whenever that great revolution swept over Camp Oro.

Felipe closed his eyes and felt a spinning dizziness take over his consciousness. As he fell into an exhausted sleep, he was smiling.

TRACK ROLLED TO THE GROUND as bullets smacked into the tree above his head. He came up in time to see Zulu dive for cover with George not a beat behind him.

Laredo's mouth exploded inward and he sat down on the ground, swaying there with a large, bloody hole under his nose before collapsing to the earth.

Rafael went down on one knee, the stock of his 30-30 Winchester split by a bullet. Another round hit him in the chest, and he collapsed forward, falling face first to the jungle floor.

Hessler had thrown his snub-nosed revolver to the ground. He held his hands over his head, screaming, "Don't shoot! Don't shoot!"

The paratroopers stepped into the clearing that bordered the riverbank. Their submachine gun muzzles smoked from the heavy fusillade they'd just fired.

The leader, a burly corporal, motioned to Track, Zulu and George. They followed his signals, keeping their hands high as they joined Hessler.

The trooper nudged Laredo's body. *"¿Porqué quizo matarte?"* he asked Track.

Track looked at Zulu. "What did he say?"

Before Zulu could answer, the soldier spoke in English. "I ask you, why he want to kill you?"

"Kill me?" Track inquired.

"Yes, you," the corporal said. "All of you—except him." He pointed to Hessler. "When he yell, they start to aim at you. But my men and me, we shoot first."

Track glared at Hessler. "You son of a bitch!"

"Never mind," the soldier said. "What you do here, huh?"

"We're a geological surveying outfit," Track said, "employed by the Peruvian government."

"Strange thing when there is murder over surveying," the soldier said. He noted the box in the launch. "What is that?"

"Our tools," Track answered.

The soldier issued some orders in Spanish. A couple of his men trotted forward. They went to the launch and started to lift the wooden box. They couldn't budge it.

"¡Es muy pesado!" one complained.

"He say it is heavy," the corporal said. He yelled over at his men, *"¡Abrela!"*

They responded by smashing it hard with their weapons. The wood splintered, and one reached inside, dragging out the packet of papers. He trotted over and handed it to his corporal.

The NCO looked at the document seal. He wasn't impressed. After shouting more orders, he waited for his men to pull everything out of the crate. When they reached the large item wrapped in a tarpaulin, they stopped.

The corporal pointed to it. "What is that?"

Track shrugged. "Tools, that's all."

"Cortala abierta," the corporal ordered.

A quick bayonet thrust did the job.

When the canvas and tar-paper wrappings were peeled back, the two soldiers yelled in astonishment. Their corporal ordered his other men to watch the four "surveyors" as he went down to the launch. When he saw the gold and jeweled object, he returned to Track.

"What is your real business, mister?"

"Surveying for oil," Track said doggedly.

The corporal struck him hard across the face. "Answer me with the truth!"

Track snarled, tensing for whatever opportunity was available. But with five submachine guns pointed at him and his friends, there was nothing he could do.

"There is a big story here, I think," the corporal said.

Track kept his cool. "It's easy to explain."

"Then you will have an opportunity to do so," the corporal said, "to Colonel Torres at Camp Oro."

15

Colonel Jorge Torres looked closely at his image in the mirror. After a careful inspection, he took the two hairbrushes he held and ran them through his thinning hair. Although his hair was cropped short on the sides and quite sparse on top, he achieved an effect of sorts. Another look and he was satisfied.

Next came the small mustache comb. He combed his trimmed mustache meticulously with the same care he would have shown a full-blown handlebar model. Then he inspected his teeth. Brushed and flossed, their whiteness was enhanced by his olive complexion. When he was satisfied with the choppers, he turned his attention to his shave. It was thorough, the heavy beard razored away until only a hint of a five o'clock shadow danced across his jaw.

He splashed on some Old Spice shaving lotion, purchased at the Fort Gulick Post Exchange in Panama. Thus, his toilet was finished. Torres took the cleaned and pressed gabardine shirt hanging up on the bathroom door behind him. He donned the garment carefully, making sure his ribbons and other military decorations were not mussed up. He walked out into the hall to the full-length mirror that was mounted on the wall there.

The uniform, tan in color, with spit-shined jump boots and shiny metal insignia was quite fancy when compared with the camouflage fatigues he usually wore. But today was a special one for Colonel Torres.

His mistress was arriving for a month-long visit.

He thought of her and rubbed his hands in anticipation of the wonderful nights of uninhibited sex that lay ahead for him. Her wanton lusts and wild passions made her better than even the most expensive whore in Lima.

Torres walked out into the living room. An orderly there, a miserable convict allowed to dress in a white waiter's jacket and long trousers, poured him a cup of hot, thick coffee. Torres, feeling damned good, took the drink and walked to the window to sip it.

He glanced at the road that led from the front of his quarters up to the vulgar little two-lane highway designated officially as *Ruta* 12. It was supposed to be macadamed, but the crooked construction engineer had taken most of the money meant for the project and sent it to a Swiss bank. Being the brother-in-law of a minor minister in the government made it possible to pull such an outrageous trick without having to fear punishment. As a result of the contractor's dishonesty, the road was only half paved and with material that had been put on only a quarter as thick as good engineering demanded. The end product was a bumpy, irregular road that turned into a long ribbon of a mudbath in the heavy rainy season.

But Torres wasn't interested in the highway. He was looking toward it in anticipation of what might be coming down it. He finished his coffee and handed the empty cup to the prisoner. *"Otra taza, por favor,"* he said.

The convict was surprised to hear the word "please" from the colonel. He wanted to keep the commandant in a good mood so he quickly poured another cup.

Torres took the cup, then dismissed the man, who scurried away to the prison kitchen before the colonel turned back into his normally ugly self.

But he needn't have feared.

Torres actually hummed to himself as he waited. Once he went back to the hall mirror to reinspect his image. Then he returned to the window. After a half hour his patience began to wear down.

"Where is that damned Zotol?" he asked himself aloud.

Torres paced back and forth for another fifteen minutes. "If that bastard turns up drunk—" He let the sentence hang as a disturbing thought crept into his mind. He spoke his fear aloud. "Maybe she isn't coming! Maybe she missed the boat! Maybe—"

The whine of a jeep motor sounded in the distance. There was the pause that always preceded a vehicle's turning off *Ruta* 12 before bouncing onto the road leading to Camp Oro.

Torres rushed to the window and eagerly peered out. Within a few moments he was rewarded with the sight of Zotol's jeep rolling into view. And a lithe young woman was seated in the passenger seat. It was she, no doubt!

When the vehicle pulled up in front of his quarters, Torres rushed out onto the small porch. He blew a kiss down to the woman and called out affectionately, *"¡Ay, mi vida! Aquí estas al fin!"*

Smiling back at him, her beauty in stark contrast to the mundane martial conveyance she was sitting in, was Ana Garanta.

TRACK AND ZULU WALKED CAREFULLY, the two tree limbs over their shoulders pressing into their flesh. Pizarro's calendar was suspended there, held into place by ropes. Neither knew how long they'd been carrying the object. They were only aware of the fatigue that each bore with soldierly stoicism. They were too proud to show the discomfort and pain they felt.

"Wait up," the corporal said. "You finish for this turn." He pointed to George and Hessler. "Now you two carry."

George, happy to relieve Zulu and Track, stepped forward to take his turn. But Hessler was not of so generous a mind. He raised his hand in an imploring gesture. "I must tell you, I am exhausted," he said.

The corporal was not in a sympathetic mood—particularly toward pint-size malingerers. He pointed to the end of the two poles opposite George. "Pick it up, pronto."

Hessler hung his head and fell to his knees. "I am beaten. I cannot do it."

"I don't want to talk to you all day," the corporal warned him. "Get to your task."

The other soldiers who made up the patrol grinned in happy anticipation of what would happen to the little man if he didn't straighten up and show some quick obedience.

But Hessler, who hated manual labor the way a teetotaler hates liquor, implored the trooper to show him mercy. "Make these *norteamericanos* do the carrying," he said, deciding to appeal to the man's patriotic side. "After all, we are both *peruvianos*. We must stick together against foreigners, no?"

The corporal stepped forward and swung his open hand hard to land on the side of Hessler's face with a resounding smack. The little man's self-control snapped. His face paled and his eyes bugged out. *"¡Idiota!"* he screamed in rage. *"¡Te mato por tu conducta grosera!"*

"¡Mensillo!" the corporal shouted back. He punctuated his displeasure by launching into a fist-swinging, boot-pounding attack that slammed Hessler to the soft jungle earth. The little man rolled in a desperate attempt to escape

the assault, but the closeness of the trees and brush around him prevented any relief.

Finally the corporal was tired. "Get up!"

Hessler struggled to his feet, rubbing his bloody nose. He slipped and fell, then quickly scrambled upright as the corporal rushed toward him again. His behavior had been modified greatly. Tears welled up in his eyes and cascaded down his plump cheeks. "Why are you so cruel to me? I never did you wrong."

The corporal kicked him again. "Pick up that end!"

Hessler nodded and limped over to the two poles. He struggled mightily with the load, but could not raise it to his shoulders.

The corporal advanced, his face grim and angry.

Hessler, anticipating more physical abuse if he didn't do as he was ordered, decided to avoid any potential physical pain. He heaved the burden up and slipped under it.

Track, despite his own weariness, grinned. "Hessler, your temper is going to get you killed one of these days."

"*¡Sangron!*" Hessler screamed. He dropped the poles and rushed at Track.

Track sidestepped the attack and grabbed the little man around the waist, lifting him up high. He carried him back to the poles and dropped him down.

Hessler hissed something unintelligible, then angrily picked up the poles and sat them on his shoulders.

"Move out!" the corporal commanded.

The little column resumed its journey through the jungle.

TORRES RAISED HIS GLASS of wine and gazed fondly over it at Ana Garanta, seated at the table opposite him. "To us, *mi vida*."

She smiled and lifted her own drink. "Yes, *mi amor*. To us!"

The two were in the small dining room of the colonel's quarters. The furniture there, despite the lack of size and elegance, was expensive. A heavy linen cloth covered the table, and the service laid was of sterling silver and fine bone china.

Ana's little maid, Lupita, stood demurely off to one side watching the proceedings. She really had nothing to do. The convict servant, dressed as usual in a white waiter's jacket over his denims, kept their wineglasses filled as the two enjoyed their repast. In ordinary circumstances, the man's eyes would have been riveted to Ana's breasts. But instead he hungrily looked at the food. Since he had been taken from the mine to perform domestic duties, his daily ration had been cut. In fact, he was getting only a bit more than men enduring *el Trato* were fed. A hungry man yearns more for sustenance than sex.

The job he performed was only temporary. After going without a decent meal, most of the servants preferred to return to hard labor in the mines. At least a man ate well as long as he performed his job properly.

Torres felt amorous and tender. He motioned the convict to leave, taking the wine from him. Lupita, not moving, stayed where she was. Her innocent eyes, wide open with curiosity and nosiness, ogled the pair.

Torres frowned at her, then made a silent, pleading gesture to Ana. The woman took the hint and smiled over at her maid. *"Tú puedes ir también, Lupita."*

"Sí, Señorita Ana." Lupita, who didn't like Torres one whit, left reluctantly.

Torres smiled. "As the Americans say, 'Two's company, three's a crowd.'"

The cliché made Ana suddenly remember Dan Track. She had made that statement to him in her dressing room at the nightclub in Lima. She sighed aloud.

Torres thought it was for him, and he was touched. The colonel poured another two glasses, then took the chair next to Ana. He smiled at her, kissing her cheek. "How I have missed you, *querida*."

"And I have longed for you, my brave soldier," Ana said.

Torres's passion was mounting higher with each glance at the woman so close to him. But he was too much of a gentleman to rush her. After all, this was no tart—she was a beautiful woman used to first-class treatment by men of high society.

He took her hand. "Shall we go to the porch, *palomita mia*," he cooed. "And look at the moon, so lovely tonight."

"Ay, Jorgecito, eres tan romántico," she said.

Torres gently led her through the small house to the porch.

Ana gazed upward. *"La luna es muy bellisima,"* she said softly.

"Yes, yes," Torres said, feeling so much in love. "The moon is indeed beautiful." He looked fondly at her. "But not so much as you, *mi dulcita*."

THE HANDCUFFS AND MANACLES had been clamped down hard on the prisoners. Track and his companions were linked by the merciless metal bonds. Dan lay on his back with Zulu on one side and Hessler on the other. The corporal had thought it wise to put the two biggest prisoners in the middle rather than have one or both on an end without the encumbrance of being chained to another man.

The soldiers had eaten an hour earlier. The only thing they gave their captives was a couple of swallows of water.

Track, Zulu and George took the tepid liquid and the rough treatment they were receiving in stride. None of the three would give the soldiers the satisfaction of seeing him in more discomfort than was absolutely necessary.

But Hessler was a bit different.

"Take away these cuffs!" he begged. "I have no circulation in my hands. Do you hear me? My hands are numb—there is no blood there! *¡Ay, Dios de mi vida!* They will rot and fall off! Please! Please! Please!"

"You are disturbing us," the corporal said as a warning.

"Must I lose my fingers!" Hessler asked, deciding to decrease his whining as a conciliatory token. "I cannot move them. Look!"

The corporal sighed and got to his feet. He walked over to the little prisoner and kicked him hard.

Hessler came unglued.

He screamed and thrashed violently in an effort to get at the soldier. Zulu, the closest to the raging gnome, tried to calm him. "Please, Hessler. You must control yourself." Zulu was also feeling a lot of discomfort. Each time Hessler leaped, the manacles pulled and bit into the African's wrists and ankles.

A short burst of machine gun fire blasted out, the bullets zipping upward into the vegetation above them.

Hessler shut up.

The corporal stood with his smoking weapon. "The next one goes into you, *chaparro*!" the corporal promised.

Hessler relaxed and lay back on the ground. He sighed, then breathed deeply as his temper subsided.

"You little shit!" George hissed at him. "Track was wrong. You ain't gonna get you killed! You're gonna get all of us bumped off!"

COLONEL JORGE TORRES and Ana Garanta were wrapped together tightly on his bed. He plunged into her, his breath heavy and loud in the small sleeping chamber.

Ana had thrown her legs over his back and locked her ankles tightly in an unconscious effort to keep him inside her until she was ready. She gritted her teeth, bit his shoulders and raked his back with her nails as she gyrated her hips frantically, trying to bring herself to climax.

By then Torres was thrusting so violently that the couple was almost bouncing up and down on the bed. He reached his peak and came in spasms, his buttocks quivering with the effort.

Ana, disappointed, felt his warm seed and the sudden softness of his manhood.

She sighed sadly.

This was the way it had been all the time lately. No matter how large or long-lasting her lovers, she had not had an orgasm since the wonderful night she had spent with the American petroleum engineer, Track.

Ana relaxed as Torres pulled out to roll over and lie beside her. The colonel turned his head and glanced at her fondly. *"Fue maravilloso,"* he said. "How was it for you?"

"Igualmente," she lied. After a moment she spoke again. "I am tired. I suppose it is from the trip and the lovemaking." She wiggled to the other side of the bed and faced the wall.

"Is there something the matter?" Torres asked.

"No, *mi vida*," she said. "It is just that I am completely worn out."

But Ana Garanta knew her plummeting spirits were caused by one thing: she was doing one of the worst things a woman could ever do to herself—lying with one man while loving another.

16

Pizarro's calendar had been placed on the chair in Torres's office. Two husky paratroopers, struggling with the heavy object, set it there under Sergeant Zotol's stern supervision.

The colonel, intrigued by the bejeweled gold object, sat at his desk across the room, gazing in near rapture at its priceless beauty.

Even the bare light bulb hanging from the ceiling made the gold and jewels sparkle. Green and ruby-colored flashes intermingled with golden reflections from the disk.

Torres recognized it as an authentic Inca relic. He also took instant and expert notice of its value. In its present state it was worth a fortune beyond belief. Even if it was melted down and the stones pried out and sold separately, it would bring a healthy price.

Torres took the pack of documents that had been packed in the crate with the calendar. He thumbed through them, noting the legal gibberish in which they had been written. They were obviously phony. The seal was outdated and the words on the documents were just so much nonsense, adding up to one thing: someone, with a pretty fair knowledge of Peruvian legal terminology, had sat down and typed out a document that neither claimed to be official, nor disclaimed it, either. It was a neutral jumble of words that would not incriminate the obvious source of the papers—the National Museum.

Torres hit the small bell on his desk.

The door to his office immediately opened and Sergeant Zotol presented himself with a sharp salute. *"¿Sí, mi coronel?"*

"Bring in the *gringo*," Torres ordered.

After a few moments Track was shoved into the room in front of a pair of armed paratroopers. The American took the rude treatment with a somber expression on his face. He displayed no fear and no arrogance. Track simply appeared nonchalant. He even affected a respectful greeting. "How do you do?"

"I am very fine, thank you," Torres replied in perfect English. He picked up the passport. "Dan Track—American."

"Yes, sir," Track said.

"May I inquire, Mr. Track, why you were running about in the Peruvian jungle with a priceless artifact from the Peruvian past?"

Track pointed to the documents on the desk. "Those explain everything."

Torres slowly shook his head. "Those explain nothing. They are just mumbo jumbo—" he laughed "—or as the Americans say, a lot of bullshit."

"Well, I wouldn't know about that," Track said. "But I'm sure this matter can be straightened out. I would appreciate it if I could be put in touch with the nearest American consulate."

"In due time, Mr. Track. Where did you get this ancient calendar?" Torres asked.

Track started to give a cover story, then thought better of it. He'd committed no crimes. He was a legal prisoner in the hands of the authorities. Better to tell the truth and let the people involved sort things out. His job had been to protect the calendar for certain member companies of The Consortium. He had done just that. Track spoke frankly. "My two friends and I represent an insurance organization that had covered the safe acquisition and retrieval of the relic. As a matter of fact, the Peruvian National Museum is involved."

"Yes," Torres agreed. "These papers are obviously from the museum."

"They explained to us they didn't want to go through normal channels because of unsavory characters in the government," Track went on.

Torres laughed aloud. "Indeed! I can't say that I blame them."

"That's it in a nutshell," Track said. "Pretty simple."

"The patrol leader that arrested you reports that your Peruvian companions were about to kill you and your two men when he intervened," Torres said.

"So it would seem."

"Any particular reason?" Torres asked.

"Greed."

"Do you feel they were out to steal the calendar?"

"Of course," Track said. "By the way, where are my two friends?"

"They are in *custodia proteccionista*," Torres replied. "That is to say, protective custody."

Track eyed the officer carefully. There was something weird about the son of a bitch, but he couldn't quite figure it out—maybe just too much time in the fucking jungle. "May I visit them please?"

"It would not be—ah, convenient," Torres said. "But do not fear for them. They are under my personal care. And so are you, Mr. Track. You will remain in the guardhouse."

"I'm a little confused," Track said. He pointed out through the window. "What type of installation is this?"

"A military prison," Torres replied. "But neither you nor Señor Hessler will be put into the general population of prisoners."

"What about my friends?" Track asked.

"They will earn their keep," Torres said. "You are dismissed, Mr. Track." He gestured to his soldiers.

Track was alarmed for Zulu and George. But he knew it would do neither him nor them any good to protest at that particular time. He allowed himself to be led away.

After he was gone, Torres called for Don Juan Hessler.

Hessler, looking worn and mistreated, eyed Torres suspiciously. He had experienced many situations with the officials of his country. "Why am I being held here, Señor Coronel?"

Torres pointed to the calendar. "Where did you get that?"

Hessler turned and looked. After gravely studying the gold object for several seconds, he returned his eyes to Torres. "The American, Track, had it."

"You were with him, *verdad*?"

Hessler hesitated; when he finally spoke he did so rapidly. "He was trying to steal one of our national treasures, and I was going to retrieve it and take it to Lima."

"Is that why you and your men were about to shoot him when my soldiers arrived on the scene?"

Hessler became enthusiastic. "Oh, yes! I had asked him—no! I had demanded, *señor*, demanded that he return the calendar. But he refused. He even insulted our country—our *bandera*, the flag!" Hessler feigned great indignation. "I was mortally insulted, and wished to avenge our honor—" He stood up straight as he'd seen soldiers do during parades. "It was my duty as a *patriota*."

Torres pulled a paper from his top desk drawer. "This is a radiogram from Lima," he explained. "Care to know what it says?"

Hessler smiled. "Why, *Coronel*, only if you wish for me to."

"It is your criminal record, Don Juan Hessler," Torres said. "You are so notorious, Hessler, that we were able to get this information in an amazingly quick time. In fact, there are several outstanding warrants for your arrest now."

"Oh, no, *mi coronel*," Hessler insisted. "There must be some mistake."

"You want to talk to me about it on *el teléfono*?" Torres asked. "Or shall we begin speaking frankly about your involvement with this ancient artifact from our nation's glorious past?"

Hessler gulped. He had undergone such interrogations on two occasions from the Policía Federal. "I got the calendar in the jungle."

"I see," Torres said. "You were simply walking along and happened to look down and see an ancient gold Inca calendar, eh?"

"I got it from a poacher," Hessler said. "His name is Correro."

"I know of him," Torres said. "He's come pretty close to getting himself thrown in here."

"Ah, yes, *Coronel*," Hessler said, displaying an expression of distaste and disapproval. "A despicable character. Really no good. Why if—"

"¡Silencio!"

Hessler shut up.

Torres motioned the two paratroopers in the room to leave. When they had shut the door, he spent a long minute simply studying Hessler's homely face.

The little man's bug eyes darted around nervously.

Finally, Torres spoke again. "Is it possible to get more of these relics?"

Hessler immediately understood. "Oh, yes, *Coronel*. Correro knows where there are many more such things. He says a tribe of Indians up the Riachuelo Verde have many objects hidden around." He exaggerated the actual situation to improve his position in dealing with the army officer.

"I have told Track that he and you will not be placed in the prison proper," Torres said. "Rather you will be confined in the soldiers' guardhouse."

"¡Muchas gracias, mi coronel!"

"I shall have to think over this situation and reach some decisions," Torres said.

Hessler knew how to grovel. "An excellent idea, *mi coronel*. In the meantime, is there something I might do for you? I have an excellent mind. I am an educated man in many things—" Hessler was getting desperate. He didn't know what the hell this army camp was, but it sure wasn't like anything he'd ever seen before. "I have certain sensibilities. Perhaps you need a skilled house servant, *mi coronel*?"

"Of course. Perhaps—" Torres stopped speaking. He suddenly thought of Track. It would certainly impress Ana if a big, strapping *yanqui* would be at his mercy. He could make Track hop, and Ana would know what an *hombre* she really had. He waved Hessler away. "You are dismissed, Hessler. I will summon you when I need you."

"*Sí, mi coronel.*" Hessler almost bowed, but the colonel banged the bell on his desk and two paratroopers instantly appeared to drag the little prisoner away.

Torres called out into the other room. "Sergeant Zotol! Bring in Track. I have a job for him."

GEORGE BEEGH RUBBED his shaved head. "Shit!"

Zulu laughed. "Now you are finally sporting the best hairdo a man can have."

The two, wearing only sandals and shorts, stood in the convict barracks. The other prisoners were eating, but the newcomers had not been allowed any food.

"Why wouldn't they feed us?" George asked.

"The soldiers said we can't eat until we've worked," Zulu explained. "It appears that means we won't have a meal until midday tomorrow."

"Damn it!" George said. "I'm so hungry, my stomach thinks my throat's been cut."

"You won't die," Zulu said. He pointed. "Look. There's a couple of empty sleeping mats over there. Let's sit down and relax. If we can't get food, we'd better store up as much energy as we can. I think that's the best policy to follow in a hard labor camp."

"No shit," George said. "Did you see all those guys coming out of that cave with shovels and picks?"

"Yes," Zulu said. "And I believe that is a mine shaft, not a cave."

"Whatever it is, it's bad news," George said. He lay down on the mat.

A few moments later, several prisoners wandered into the barracks. One, a wiry, dark man, took his place next to George. He nodded in a friendly matter. *"Buenas noches."*

"Buenas noches," Zulu responded.

"How're you doing?" George said.

The man sat up. "You speak English! You Americans?"

"I am," George said. He indicated Zulu. "This guy's from Africa, but he speaks English too."

"The Queen's English," Zula emphasized.

The prisoner offered his hand. "I am Antonio Poreso, a Mexican." He winked at George. "I know your country well. They throw me outta there many, many times."

"What are you, undesirable or something?" George asked dryly.

"Illegal alien," Poreso said. "But a hardworking fellow at stoop labor, man!"

Another convict approached them and stretched out on the pallet on the other side of Poreso. He was a youngster, but there was something hard about his face that belied his age. Poreso introduced him as Felipe Rodriguez.

Felipe, learning George was an American, showed some mild interest. He mumbled something in Spanish. Poreso translated the words. "He say you are the first American he ever see."

"There's another one here," George explained. "The toughest son of a bitch you'll ever come across. His name is Dan Track." He pointed to Zulu. "And this guy can kick some ass, too, believe me."

Poreso did some more translating. Felipe showed an increase in interest. He studied Zulu more closely. This, indeed, was a formidable man. George, also, displayed a healthy, strong physique. "You fellows will last a long time in here," Felipe said in Spanish.

Zulu laughed, but George wasn't amused when the words were translated. "Tell him," he said to Zulu, "that we ain't staying here long. If they don't turn us out, we'll fight our way out."

Felipe had heard empty boasts before, but this one seemed genuine. "Who is the other American we've yet to see?" he asked.

"My uncle," George explained. "He's plenty tough, believe me, brother. In fact, they won't even let him in here with the rest of us. They're afraid he'll start a prison break, man! It'd be like Spartacus leading a slave revolt."

Zulu cautioned his young friend. "You don't know why Dan isn't with us, George. You'll make him look pretty silly if he suddenly shows up in the barracks here and announces we've been released."

George shook his head. "Don't fool yourself, Zulu. Those guys running this place can recognize a badass when they see one. If they turn Dan loose in this compound, you can bet they'll keep a close eye on him." He smirked. "Dan's been a prisoner before—and in tougher situations than this one. There's no way to hold him if he wants out."

Poreso did some quick talking to Felipe to let him know what the two new fellows had said. Felipe was, most assuredly, impressed. He looked into Poreso's eyes. *"Posiblemente, aquél Señor Track es nuestro libertador."*

"What'd he say?" George asked.

Zulu answered, "He said that maybe Track is the liberator."

George smiled viciously. He winked at Felipe. "You bet your ass he is!"

Poreso was no optimist. He quickly crossed himself. "I think that *El Muerte*—Death—has walked into Camp Oro this day."

"There's a saying in America," George interjected. "I'd rather die on my feet than live on my knees."

Antonio Poreso looked grimly into George's face. "Colonel Torres will give you the opportunity to die in any position you want!"

17

Track stood outside the door of the guardhouse. The paratrooper watching him was impressed by the American's build and size. The soldier instinctively kept his submachine gun muzzle high.

Track was dressed in some of his own freshly laundered clothing. He wore a white T-shirt and olive-drab fatigue trousers. His bare feet were encased in a pair of prison-issue sandals. They had tried to get him to wear a starched waiter's jacket, but the only sizes they had were too small for his broad shoulders.

When he was first informed he'd been detailed to act as a servant in Colonel Torres's quarters, Track had been tempted to show his resentment—by slamming the corporal's ass up between his ears—but after some calm consideration, he saw the situation as an opportunity to get a pretty good look at the layout of the place.

His guard, a short, tough paratrooper, gestured toward the gate of the barbed-wire fence surrounding the guardhouse. Track acted docile, following the hand signals as he left the area and was pushed over to the building where the colonel lived.

"*Ya arriba,*" the soldier said, shoving him up the steps of the back porch.

Track smiled at the soldier and spoke in a friendly tone. "One of these days, you little fucker, I'm going to squeeze your head just to see the shit come out of your ears."

Not understanding but sensing the animosity from the big man, the trooper opened the back door and ordered Track through it with a motion of his hand.

Lupita turned at the sound of the entrance. When the little Indian woman saw Track, her eyes opened wide. *"¡Ay Dios!"* she exclaimed.

ZULU'S PICK DUG into the earthen wall with rhythmic regularity. The black man's body glistened with perspiration and his corded muscles knotted with the effort of each blow of the tool. After a dozen strokes he stepped back and allowed George to scoop up the earth he'd dug out. The younger man dumped it into a waiting wheelbarrow.

George worked and talked at the same time. He had to speak low, however. The guards cautioned him a couple of times about unnecessary conversation. "So this is a gold mine, huh?"

"It sure is," Zulu whispered.

George lifted his shovel and heaved a load of dirt into the wheelbarrow. "I guess that bartender Jimmy in Rio Vista was right when he said there were old Incan mines out here in the boonies."

"It stands to reason," Zulu said, taking up his pick for another go at the mine wall. "Those ancients had to get the precious metal someplace."

"Yeah," George agreed. He glanced around at the other miners laboring with hand tools. "Why don't these fuckers bring in some machinery and do this job right?"

Zulu shook his head between blows of the pick. "That is very strange," he mused. "In fact, there's something about this prison that doesn't quite ring true."

"I agree," George said. "There's a real weird atmosphere about it. It's like everyone here is going to stay till they die."

"Indeed," Zulu said. "There's another ominous thing."

"What's that?" George asked.

"The sign on the front gate says, *Se Gana Libertad por Trabajo*. That means one earns freedom through work."

"Doesn't sound ominous to me," George said.

"It does when you consider that on the front gate of Auschwitz concentration camp, the Germans had a sign that said *Arbeit Mach Frei*."

"What if I conclude that that means the same thing in German?"

"Then your conclusion would be correct," Zulu said. He stepped back.

George's scoop shovel slipped into the newly dug-out earth. "Don't tell me these bastards have gas chambers here!"

"Probably not," Zulu said. "But I would wager they have other methods just as deadly."

"The dirty sons of bitches better not—"

"¡Silencio!" The guard's loud voice echoed through the man-made chamber of dirt.

George gritted his teeth and whispered, "This bears some looking into."

Zulu used one of the young American's own expressions. "No shit!"

TRACK QUICKLY RAISED his fingers to his lips.

Lupita, puzzled and surprised, was still able to react to the subtle signal. She dropped her gaze to the floor, then turned and went back to her work of preparing a serving tray.

The paratrooper who'd brought Track into the house poured himself a cup of coffee from the stove, then settled down on a stool in the corner.

When Lupita finished her work, she turned to Track with a shy smile. *"Esta listo, señor."* She pointed to the tray.

Track glanced at it and saw a couple of empty cups, a sterling silver teapot and a small plate of cookies. From her gestures he finally was able to understand that he was to take it into the next room.

And Dan Track knew damn well who was in there.

He picked up the load and walked to the door, hoping that Ana Garanta would not cry out when he entered. In order to avoid an instant shock, he backed into the door, then eased out into the next room. Then he slowly turned.

Ana Garanta most certainly did cry out. *"¿Qué es esto?"*

She was seated on the sofa in the living room. Beside her, wearing a standard set of fatigues, Colonel Torres smiled at her in a patronizing manner. "Have no fear, Ana, my love," he said in English. "This man is only another prisoner here."

Ana, also given a subtle sign by Track—he gave his head a slight negative shake—put her hand to her breast. She looked at Torres with a quizzical expression on her face. *"No entiendo,"* she said.

"Tut, tut, my dear," Torres said. "Let us speak English for the sake of the prisoner." He glared meaningfully at Track. "And, Mr. Track, you are a prisoner. Do you understand that."

Track had decided to cool it right away. "Yeah."

"That is not the proper manner to speak to me!" Torres snapped.

Track smiled. "Yes, sir."

"Ah! Yes, that is better," Torres said. "The lady here speaks English and will be able to give you instructions about what she wishes."

Ana Garanta knew damned well what she wished with Track. But she, like him, put a damper on her emotions. "Yes. I am able to talk at him."

"Excellent," Torres said. He sat back on the sofa and pointed to the coffee table. "Serve us, Track."

"Yes, sir."

Ana fought to keep her eyes off the handsome face. All she allowed herself were a few quick glances.

After Track had poured the coffee, he stepped back and stood silently a few steps away from the couple. Being a waiter was something he had never done before. But Torres was ready with instructions. "Don't gape at us, Track. Go over there by the door. I will snap my fingers when I need you."

Track, who had been staring down the front of Ana's dress, made a slight bow. This gave him a better look at the full breasts beneath the thin material. It also served to put Torres off guard about any ideas the American might have had about putting up resistance. Track, who would have preferred to stomp Torres's ass good and proper, denied himself that pleasure—for the moment. He even smiled again, and said, "Yes, sir."

Track walked over by the door where he'd entered, to stand silently awaiting any summons. From his vantage point he could get a good look at Ana's fantastic legs. He'd have been willing to bet his Franchi SPAS-12 assault shotgun against a Daisy BB gun that the colonel would have shit himself then and there had he known that Track was familiar with everything Ana had under her skimpy dress.

"My job is like a lion tamer's," Torres said to Ana. "The men in here are tough as nails, believe me, but I must prove to them who is the master—the absolute master. When they learn that I am in complete command, most buckle down quickly enough. Those that don't—" He affected a little laugh. "Well, my dear, I do not wish to offend your sensitive ears with the unpleasantries they endure before breaking to my will."

"You are a natural leader, Jorge," Ana said. She bent forward for another sip of coffee. As she reached for her cup, she glanced at Track. She wanted the stud between her legs so bad she could taste it. She took a sip of the hot brew. "Of course, if you're out of sight, they do as they please, no?"

Track grinned to himself. The woman was playing a psychological game with the megalomaniac, milking his ego to her own benefit.

"Of course not!" Torres protested. "My presence is as strong in spirit as it is physically."

"You mean to say," Ana said sweetly, "that the big American would be as docile without you being here?"

"Of course!" Torres leaned forward and gestured at Track. "Come here, *gringo*!"

Track scurried over. "Yes, sir?"

"You are to be the house servant here on a permanent basis, understand?"

"When may I speak to the nearest American consulate?"

"When I say so, damn it!" Torres shouted. "If you anger me, you will never, never, never see it!"

"Oh, please, sir," Track said.

Torres calmed down. "In the meantime, make yourself available to Doña Ana. Can you say, 'Doña Ana'?"

"Doña Ana," Track mimicked.

"Not bad," Torres said, getting up. He went to the coatrack by the door and took his red beret from it. He smiled at Ana. "I have business to attend to. Remember that Track is at your service. If he happens to give you any trouble, just yell out to the kitchen. There is a soldier there."

"Oh, sir," Track said. "You won't need a soldier here. All I want is to get my situation straightened out and dealt with properly."

Ana frowned. "I don't like your soldiers, Jorge. They are so unpleasant."

Torres laughed. "Of course, my darling. I will leave through the kitchen and dismiss him." He turned a hard stare at Track. "Remember! Do what she wants of you!"

"Yes, sir. Of course."

The colonel kissed Ana on the cheek, then went out to the kitchen.

Ana, her eyes sultry and demanding, turned to face Track. "You know what I want, Dan!" she whispered eagerly.

GEORGE BEEGH DIPPED into the palm-frond dish and picked out a bit of fish with his fingers. He ate it slowly and thoughtfully.

He and Zulu, along with Felipe Rodriguez and Antonio Poreso, were seated along the wall of the mine in their work area. The kitchen crew had just passed through, leaving them with steamed fish, fresh fruit and cool water as a midday repast.

George finally spoke. "I'm worried about Dan."

"Me, too," Zulu said. "I don't like not hearing from him after so much time."

Poreso translated their words for Felipe. After a few moments of speaking together, the Mexican nudged Zulu. "Felipe, he say you no worry for your friend, eh?"

"And why not?" George demanded.

"Because," Poreso explained, "when they do something bad to somebody here, ever'body he got to watch. Is for to teach lessons to the others. Understand?"

"You're probably right," Zulu said.

"Sure," George said, brightening. "I'll bet that commandant guy is pretty worried now." He laughed. "Now he knows what it's like to grab a tiger by the tail."

Poreso told Felipe what they said. Felipe said something, and Poreso translated it. "Felipe, he say, you tell your friend to come on in. Then, when he is ready to fight, tell Felipe. We have the big *revolución*, eh?"

"No shit!" George said.

"Frankly, George," Zulu said somberly, "I don't share your enthusiasm. I'm very worried about the unpleasant things that Dan might be going through at this very moment!"

ANA GARANTA'S FINGERS were entwined in Track's hair. Her eyes were tightly closed and she gasped loudly as her arms and legs clasped his body close to her own.

Naked, the two were intertwined tightly in the lovers' embrace on Torres's bed. This was their third coupling since the colonel had taken his leave two and a half hours previously.

Ana had reached the peak of release each time, but she had yet to experience full satisfaction. Her passions returned after a short time, as her seemingly insatiable sexual appetite continued to make demands on Track's male prowess.

But this time, she had reached complete fulfillment.

She bit and scratched him through the spasms of relief as her hands pressed on his muscular buttocks to keep him deep within her for as long as possible.

Her gasping had gone to loud cries, then tapered off to blissful silence as she felt the first satisfaction she'd known since bedding with him in Lima.

Finally, untangling themselves, the two lay side by side, taking in air in slow, deep breaths. Finally Ana was normal again. She turned her head and looked at Track. "Why are you here in this prison, Dan?"

He grinned at her. "Finally decided to opt for some conversation, huh?"

"Don't make fun for me," she pouted. "And answer my question. Why you here?"

"A mix-up," he explained. "The authorities will straighten it out and my friends and I will be on our way."

Ana sat up. "No! Dan, listen to me! This is no a regular prison. Nobody outside knows about it."

Track frowned in confusion. "Are you saying this isn't an official installation?"

"It belongs to Jorge Torres. No prisoners ever leave here," she said.

Track felt sudden agitation. "Could you explain a little more about what the hell are you talking about?"

Ana spoke rapidly. She told him of what little she knew. No one in the government knew about the prison. It was a private enterprise of Torres's, and a part of some grandiose scheme he was hatching. She only knew bits and pieces from listening to his boasts and conversations with Sergeant Zotol. She ended her story with an understatement:

"You got to get away from here, Dan."

Track looked at her. "I'll need help—your help."

"Okay, Dan." She smiled at him. "Then you marry me, eh?"

"We'll talk about it."

"No. You promise to marry me, or I won't help you for nothing!"

Track sighed. He looked around the stark quarters and through a slit in the curtains to the prison yard outside. His mind spoke to him of his deepest regrets:

I knew I was gonna get fucked up on this mission!

18

Sergeant Emiliano Zotol sat silently in his commander's office, watching the colonel ponder on the situation that had arisen since the newcomers' arrival.

Zotol was a bit tired, but he knew there was something important gnawing at the colonel's mind. The sergeant glanced outside into the prison compound.

It was evening. The gasoline lanterns had been lit by the guards as per operating procedure. Zotol turned his attention back to the colonel.

Finally Torres spoke. "I have great faith in your intuition, *Sargento*. Which one do we work with?"

"I do not trust Track or Hessler, *mi coronel*," Zotol said. "The little man is a thief and a petty criminal. There's not an army barracks in the world that doesn't have one or two crafty bastards like him. Yet, because of his underworld connections, he might be quite valuable to us."

"I agree," Torres said. "There is no doubt that he approached the Museo Nacional and impressed the staff enough that they believed him about Pizarro's calendar." He looked over at the golden object. "It is thought to be no more than a legend, yet here it is."

Zotol shrugged. "I have never heard of it."

"We studied about it in school," Torres said. "Most historians had reached the conclusion that it was only a wild tale that old conquistadores told to impress younger generations."

"What do you think of the *gringo* Track?" Zotol asked.

"A paper tiger," Torres said with a laugh.

"I don't know about that," Zotol said. He judged other men by how he would approach them in a fistfight on the drill field. If he had to square off against Track, he would be damn nervous about it, and start off the fight with some of the dirtiest tricks he knew. "The *gringo* and his friends had some pretty impressive weapons."

"They must be for show," Torres concluded. "Track is working in my house as one of the most docile prisoner servants I have ever had."

Zotol shook his head slowly. "It is hard to believe."

"Yes. But true," Torres assured him. "He's not particularly efficient, I fear. Ana was out of sorts when I arrived home earlier this afternoon. She didn't want anything to do with me. I know it's because she's upset because of Track's ineptitude."

"Are you going to send him to the mine?" Zotol asked.

"No. He shall continue his servant duties. But I'm removing him from the guardhouse so that he and Hessler will not see each other. Track can sleep in the prisoner barracks. He amuses me, and I'm sure Ana is impressed with the power I have over the big man. And besides, Track is an American who must also have connections," Torres said. "But I can't quite figure them out. He also is working through the museum, yet he is a foreigner."

"Perhaps he is planning on moving the calendar to the United States," Zotol suggested.

Torres liked that idea. "There would be more money there than with the Museo Nacional."

Zotol, a real movie fan, had another thought. "Perhaps, *mi coronel*, Track had an arrangement with the Mafia."

Torres started to scoff, then thought better of it. In a way, Zotol made sense. "You could be absolutely right, *Sargento.* Or perhaps some eccentric American millionaire has an interest in Pizarro's calendar, eh?"

"I suggest we keep an eye on both Track and Hessler," Zotol said. "When we have decided which one to deal with, we will put the other into the prison."

Torres shook his head. "I think not, *Sargento*. Both are risks in their own way. The one we reject is the one who dies."

"What if it is Track? We have two of his friends in confinement," Zotol reminded him.

"El Trato," Torres said, "for all three."

THE GUARD GAVE TRACK as hard a shove as he could. But the big man only stumbled forward a couple of steps before going through the barracks door. The American turned and looked closely around the oblong room. The other prisoners, surprised by the size and physique of the big man, stared back at him for several seconds before respectfully dropping their eyes.

"Dan!"

Track looked down the row of sleeping mats and saw George Beegh and Hodari Zulu. He walked down to them, then stopped short at seeing George. "What the hell did they do to your hair?"

"The sons of bitches cut it off," George complained.

"He looks better, I think," Zulu said. "He always kept his skull cropped close."

Track laughed. "He looks like a ripe melon."

George frowned. "It ain't funny, man."

Track laughed harder. "If you had warts, you'd look like a cantaloupe."

George shook his head. "Well, now, you're in a good mood. As a matter of fact, you sound like you just got laid."

"I did," Track said, settling down with his friends.

"Knock off the bullshit, man," George said. "And how'd you get to keep your hair? Look around. Every poor bastard in here is as bald as an egg."

"I don't think they've quite figured out what my role is in the calendar caper," Track said. "They probably want to keep me presentable until they figure things out." He suddenly turned at the approach of two strangers.

Felipe Rodriguez and Antonio Poreso had left their own mats and joined the three friends. Zulu introduced Track to them.

Felipe edged nearer to the American and examined him closely. *"¡Seguro!"* he exclaimed. *"Aquí es nuestro jefe."*

"What'd he say?" Track asked.

"He said it's for sure that you're our leader," Zulu said. "This little guy is quite anxious to take leave of these lovely surroundings."

"I can't imagine why," Track said. He gave Felipe a careful look in the lantern light. He was a young kid but he had an aged, tough face. "This guy's been through some shit!"

Antonio Poreso gave Felipe's story in his broken English. When he'd finished, Track regarded the kid in a new light. "You want to *salir*, huh?" Track asked. "Get out of here?"

Felipe grinned through his battered mouth, and spoke the only English word he knew. "Yes."

Track, always watchful for spies and snitches in any situation, was satisfied with both Felipe and Poreso. There was no doubt the two had not been planted in the prison population as agents. Chicken-shit informers don't go through the hell necessary to acquire the scars and calluses that those two had. He was also sure they could keep their mouths shut.

Antonio Poreso was anxious and impatient. "What are we to do now, chief?"

"Stay cool and keep out of trouble," Track advised him. "When the time is right, we'll move—and move fast. I don't want anybody beaten up and hurting, got it?"

Zulu was surprised by Track's words. "I say, Dan. Why are you speaking of a prison break when we've yet to present our case to the authorities?"

But George, ever enthusiastic, sensed a situation ripe with impending action. "What's going on, Dan? You act like something's in the mill already."

"This is no regular prison," Track said. "And it looks like we're completely at the mercy of the commandant."

"How did you find that out?" Zulu wanted to know.

"A very reliable source," Track said. "You're going to find out about it sooner or later, so I want you prepared," Track said. "Ana Garanta is the prison commandant's guest."

"Oh, shit!" George exclaimed. "Damn you, Dan Track. You did get laid."

Track grinned and shrugged. "It's a tough job, but somebody's got to do it."

DIRTY, BLACK SMOKE drifted off the homemade candles in the jungle hut. The occupants of the flimsy structure had no fuel for modern lanterns, but even if they had, they wouldn't have used them. The smoke kept the insects at bay.

These people, all men, were strikingly similar in appearance and dress. But this was not so unusual for individuals who share the same ancestral origins and the same profession—banditry.

They were wiry and short, and their gnarled hands and dark skin spoke of the hardship of their lives. Several sported scars, and others limped or were minus limbs from misadventures encountered while following their trade.

Inside, deep in their psyche, they were tough too. All had known danger and death. Even their births in the small jungle villages had been chancy affairs. There wasn't one of them whose parents hadn't lost at least half the babies they brought into the world.

Thus, taking risks didn't bother them. After all, when stealing from other men, one must expect some spirited resistance and even an encounter involving revenge. If a bandit died, there were no regrets:

Así es la vida y la muerte—such is life and death.

But when there was a serious threat in which a bandit's livelihood was threatened to the extent that his woman and children suffered, he had to take drastic action.

That was the reason for the meeting that night in the village of San Pasqual.

The mayor, a portly fellow named Ramirez, was well respected by the others. Although he was fat and out of shape, he'd done plenty of hell-raising in his day to earn the sincere esteem of his fellows. A policeman's bullet in the knee had locked his leg into perpetual stiffness. After that, he'd turned his efforts to the commercial side of thievery, by peddling the things his compatriots brought in from raids. He turned into a shrewd businessman. Everyone prospered and things were good for the village of San Pasqual.

Then the paratroopers came.

Too many men had died or disappeared. The local economy took a nosedive and hard cash became scarce. Then, when items needed for barter also fell into short supply, it was time for action—drastic action.

Ramirez lit a cigar. He exhaled the smoke and looked over the dozen men scattered about the small expanse of the hut. "So," he said. "This is all that's left of the brave *hombres* of San Pasqual."

One of the bandits, a tough little guy named Chapulin, spit on the floor. "It was the story of those damned caiman hides that drew us into Rio Vista. I would like to know who brought that tale back to us in the first place?"

"It was Martinez," a man named Leone answered. "And he died in the attack, remember?"

"Seguro," Chapulin answered. "I saw his body floating down the Amazon. I also saw something else. And I told *el alcalde* Ramirez about it."

"Yes," Ramirez said. "The soldiers took away several of our men."

Another bandit stood up. "Why did you two not tell us this before?"

"I would not allow Chapulin to say anything," Ramirez said. "Because I knew you would all rush after them. I let you know now, because you have cooled off enough to form a good plan."

The man was agitated. "You should have told us before, *Alcalde*! Who were the men?"

Chapulin answered him. "My cousin Ricardo was one. Then there was Pedro Puentes, Roberto Garcia, Joselito Negron, Carlos Jimenez and Felipe Rodriguez."

"Felipe Rodriguez?" Leone asked. "Wasn't his cousin, Flaco, with him?" He looked at the mayor. "He worked for you, *Alcalde*."

"Yes. You all know how frail he was," Ramirez explained. "But he wanted to go on at least one raid in his life. It was his last. Nobody knows what happened to him."

"I saw him and Felipe Rodriguez head for the north out of Rio Vista," somebody volunteered. "Maybe Flaco is in jail, too."

"No," Chapulin said. "I was hiding in the brush near the river dock. I saw all the fellows there. Flaco was not one of them."

A man named Placido, who was slightly drunk, stood weaving in the back of the crowd. Although only five feet eight inches in height, he was the tallest man there. "Let's stop talking about who was where and with whom," he demanded. "Our families will starve unless we drive the soldiers away."

"But can we do that?" Leone asked.

"Of course!" Placido yelled. "Remember the tale our grandfathers told of the *Emboscada Grande* when a hundred soldiers died? The army went away and never came back for twenty years. Ask Abuelo."

All eyes turned to an incredibly old fellow seated in the corner. Bent and wrinkled, the ancient man still had a feisty look in his wizened face. All the bandits quieted down to hear what he had to say.

"*Es verdad*—it is true," Abuelo said. "We had fought the soldiers in two battles before. They chased us into the jungle. We knew which way they would come so we waited for them. They were cocky and stupid. They stayed on a narrow trail and walked under our guns. I myself fired my pistol until the barrel was too hot to touch."

"Bah!" Leone snorted. "These soldiers we face are special. They do not like trails. The *paracaidistas-casadores* melt into the jungle like leopards—and in the spotted uniforms they wear, they look like them."

Placido was not discouraged. "Then I say we also become one with the rain forest. We were born here, *por Dios*! This is our country. We must fight for it now. We are doing more than robbing for goods. Our machismo is challenged."

The talk was going the way Ramirez wanted. He raised his hands for quiet. "*Bien, muchachos*. You have the spirit. Let us now settle down for serious talk of how we are going to rid ourselves—and our land—of this scourge sent to us by the government in Lima."

Chapulin, as brave as any man in the hut, was also a realist. "If we fail, we die," he reminded his friends.

"I will not fail," Placido said. "I do not mind dying. But I will not have my wife raped by soldiers."

"Yes!" Ramirez said. "And that is exactly what will happen if this war is lost."

The group yelled out in anger, but Leone calmed them down. "Let us listen to the *alcalde*. His wisdom and courage have never failed us in the past."

Ramirez, glad for the support, took a deep breath. Then he began to outline the plan that had been brewing in his mind since the Rio Vista disaster.

19

Breakfast in the colonel's quarters was a strained affair.

Ana Garanta, quiet and withdrawn, gave her full attention to the plate of fish and eggs in front of her. She ate absentmindedly, poking at the food while lost deep in reverie.

Jorge Torres, his appetite nonexistent, looked across the table at her with a soulful pleading in his eyes. After several minutes he spoke with a tone of concern in his voice. "What is the matter, *querida*? You must tell me."

Ana didn't answer him. Her drifting thoughts filled her mind with pictures of what the afternoon would bring—a violent coupling with Dan Track's muscular body.

"Mi amor," Torres said. "Please answer me."

"Pardon me?" She looked up at him with an innocent expression.

"You are not even listening!" Torres exclaimed. "I must know what is the matter. You were cold to me last night."

She smiled condescendingly. "Oh, Jorge. You know that sometimes a woman is not in the mood."

Torres shook his head. "I have never known you to not want to make love, *mi vida*."

Ana frowned involuntarily as she remembered the pawing she had gone through the previous night. Torres's hands had been all over her.

"Perhaps you are too much of a man for me," she suggested coyly. "You are such a stallion—a rutting, insatiable *caballo*!"

He smiled modestly. "Well—perhaps I am. But I yearn for you, *querida*! My body, even my soul burns for your beauty. You must not refuse me tonight. Do you promise?"

But Ana was once again lost in her thoughts of Dan Track.

Torres sighed aloud. "Please, Ana, listen—"

A loud knocking on the door interrupted him. Torres waited several moments as the disturbance continued. Then he bellowed loudly. "Track! Track!"

Track stepped through the door from the kitchen. "Yes, sir?"

"Listen to that infernal pounding! Go answer it, you idiot!"

"Yes, sir." Track walked to the door and opened it.

Sergeant Zotol hurried past the American and presented himself to the colonel with a snappy salute. "I have news, *mi coronel*!"

Torres was pissed off. *"¡Tiene que estar importante! Dime lo que es!"*

"Of course, it is important, sir," Zotol said. "We have received a communication from our post in Rio Vista that the Panhard has arrived and is being driven here immediately."

Track, unable to understand the Spanish, stood by passively.

Torres, smiling widely, leaped to his feet. "At last! We'll give it a good test." He walked around the table and hurriedly kissed Ana on the cheek. "I shall see you later, *querida*."

Ana, purposely avoiding looking at Track, gave her full attention to the colonel. "I shall count every minute."

"Don't forget your promise," Torres reminded her. Then he led Zotol out of the small house.

Track looked at Ana. "What was that all about?"

Instead of answering him, she leaped from her chair and rushed the big man, throwing her arms around him. "Oh, God damn, Track. Let's go for the bed, eh? I am too hot to make wait."

Track kissed her, clamping his hands on her firm buttocks. "What went on between Zotol and Torres?"

"Oh!" she said angrily. "I don't know. He say something is at Rio Vista. It coming here for to look at. They call it a—a—*pan duro*—hard bread."

"No. A Panhard," Track said. He smiled. "Hell! A Panhard is the name of a series of French armored vehicles. I wonder what that bastard has gotten his hands on—and I'd also like to know what he's planning on doing with it."

"Don't think on that!" Ana insisted. She pulled Track toward the bedroom.

TORRES WORKED THE STACK of papers on his desk. These were the endless reports and accountings his brigade headquarters demanded of him. Under normal circumstances, such administrative details were burdensome to a field commander. In Torres's case, since he was also covering up his real activities, the chore was close to overwhelming.

He scanned each word, making sure no slip had been made that would catch the quick eye of the alert adjutant in Iquitos. The slightest mistake could cause a surprise visit by the inspector general, and blow open his scheme.

Torres concentrated on the dreary task until the distant whine of an approaching motor interrupted his thoughts. He laid down his pen and left the desk. After grabbing his red beret, he went outside.

Zotol, standing at the headquarters steps, was waiting for him. "The APC is coming, *mi coronel.*"

"Yes," Torres acknowledged. "I heard it."

The arrival of the armored vehicle was more than just an ordinary occurrence. Skillful double dealing—and more paperwork games—had brought about a payoff to the quartermaster general of the armored corps. Using maneuvers as an excuse, the officer had arranged for the transfer of an armored personnel carrier from its regular unit to Torres's area of operations.

There had been more bribery as a couple of transportation corps officers—with their sergeants—and a civilian railroad superintendent were enlisted in the effort.

The end result was the timely arrival of a fighting vehicle good for use on either land or water.

When the machine rounded the bend in the road and came into view, both Torres and Zotol gasped in pleased surprise.

The driver, a member of the armored corps, brought the vehicle to a halt. He climbed out and reported properly. As a sergeant loyal to his captain, he'd been trusted to make the delivery in the illegal deal.

Torres returned the salute. He and Zotol walked around the armored beauty, admiring it. The colonel turned to the driver. "Well, *Sargento*, tell me all about this machine you drove in."

"Yes, *Coronel*," the NCO replied. "It is an amphibious armored personnel carrier. Its top land speed is one hundred kilometers per hour. On water it can attain at least four kilometers per hour depending on the current."

"Interesting!" Torres said.

The sergeant continued his spiel. Torres and Zotol learned that the engine was a ninety-horsepower Panhard Model 4 HD. The armor was eight millimeters thick in the minimum and twelve millimeters at the maximum. This particular model had a turret-mounted 7.62-millimeter MAS-52 machine gun.

"How many men are needed to operate it?" Zotol interjected.

"A crew of two—a driver and a gunner," the sergeant answered. "And up to ten infantrymen can be carried."

Torres gleefully rubbed his hands together. "This is what we need."

Zotol pointed over to their motor pool, where standard military vehicles—quarter-ton scout cars and two-and-a-half-ton trucks—were parked. "A couple dozen of the Panhards will replace all those."

"And we can use them on the river, too," Torres reminded him.

ANA GARANTA WAS SATISFIED. She lay on the bed wearing only a thin housecoat. She languidly smoked a cigarette, letting the smoke drift up toward the ceiling.

Track relaxed beside her. He had pulled on his trousers and slipped back into the prison sandals. If Torres showed up unexpectedtly, all he had to do was put on his T-shirt and hotfoot it back to the kitchen.

Lupita, manning her assigned post by the living room window, displayed the devotion of a loyal soldier. She kept a close eye on the garrison area. There was only one direction for the colonel to come in order to return to his house. He would never be able to do it without the little Indian woman seeing him.

Ana turned her eyes toward Track and smiled at him. "You make me happy, you know?"

"You make me happy too," Track said.

Ana snuffed out her cigarette in the ashtray on the bedstand. Then she sat up. "Now we have serious talk, Dan. You got to go away from here, no?"

"You're damn right," Track said. "There's no way that Torres is going to put me in touch with the American consulate if he wants to keep this private prison of his a secret. And that goes for my two friends, too."

"Okay," Ana said. "You tell me what to do and I help. But don't you forget, you promise for to marry me when you free."

Track nodded his head. He knew any reluctance on his part might queer the only chance that he, Zulu and George had of getting the hell out of the Amazon basin in one piece. He turned his thoughts from any future matrimonial entanglements to the job ahead.

"The first thing I need," he said, "is to get my weapon back."

"I know where are the guns," Ana said. "Jorge show me everything here. It is building on the other side of the—the *cárcel*—you know, the place where the bad soldiers stay."

"The guardhouse," Track said. "Yeah. I saw the armory when I was being kept locked up in the garrison area. But I'll have to break in there."

"No," Ana said. She slipped off the bed and went across the room to the closet. The woman opened the door and pulled out a small metal ring loaded down with a dozen keys. "These will open all important doors—Jorge he tell me this."

Track joined her and took them from her. "None are labeled, damn it! But I guess it's not worth complaining about."

"He keep them there all the time. They are extras," Ana explained. "You take, he won't know they are gone because he never use them. He has more in his office."

Track kissed her. "You're a doll!"

"You can escape Torres, Track," she said. "But you never get away from me, eh? So you remember—when you go, I go." She narrowed her eyes. "Or there be a lot of trouble for you, understand?"

"Look, Ana, I got to play this by ear," Track explained. "So I can't tell you exactly how I'm going to pull this off. But my word is good. When I go, you'll go, too."

"And Lupita, too," she reminded him.

"Yes, yes. Lupita, too."

Track knew he faced a formidable task. It would have been hairy as hell just for him to escape alone. Getting Zulu and George in on it, too, made things a hell of a lot more complicated. Then add in the two women and the odds against escalated.

"Oh, shit!" Track suddenly exclaimed, remembering that the two prisoners, Felipe Rodriquez and Antonio Poreso, would be coming along, too.

"What's the matter?" Ana asked anxiously.

"Nothing, " Track responded. Then he laughed a little. "Know where I can rent a Greyhound bus?"

ZULU TOOK a final, heavy swing at the mine wall. He stepped back to allow George to scoop up the dirt he had dug loose.

"This shit's monotonous," George said. He lazily pushed the shovel into the gold-bearing earth.

"¡Andale!" The guard's voice boomed over George's shoulder. *"¡Trabajas masrapido, cabrón!"*

George looked at Zulu. "What'd he say?"

"He told you to hurry it up," Zulu translated.

George turned and faced the soldier. "Hey, shithead! I'm doing the job, all right? Don't get fucking pushy."

The paratrooper didn't understand the words, but he could read the meaning in the young American's tone. *"Cuida la boca,"* he snarled.

Zulu was alarmed. "Do calm yourself, George. I'm afraid that bloke is about to piss himself."

George, mad as hell, threw the shovel down. He pointed a finger at the guard. "You want to step outside and see if you can back up that big mouth of yours with your ass?" He gestured to Zulu. "Tell him what I said."

"Please, George!" Zulu pleaded. "Remember what Dan advised about staying out of trouble."

"I know what he told us, man. But he didn't mean I had to kiss up to some son of a bitch!" George snapped. "Now you tell that smart-assed bastard what I said."

The guard pointed to the shovel. *"¡Agarralo, pronto!"* Then he stepped forward and slapped George hard across the face.

"You lousy bastard!" George growled. He started to charge the soldier, but Zulu grabbed him up in his muscular arms. The big African held on to the struggling young man.

"I say, George," Zulu complained, "you're worse than Hessler!"

A corporal, who had heard the commotion from his post in another chamber, suddenly appeared. He brought up his submachine gun and aimed it dead on George and Zulu.

Both immediately calmed down and raised their hands. *"Todo esta bien ahora,"* Zulu said with a smile in an effort to ease the tension.

But the corporal was not in a forgiving mood. A breach of discipline needed a quick answer. He motioned for George to precede him out of the mine.

The other paratrooper watched them leave. Then he laughed and spoke to Zulu. *"Negro, tu amigo va a la Caja de Suda."*

Zulu grimaced. Although his Spanish was not perfect, he knew the meaning of those last words:

Caja de Sudar—Sweat Box!

20

Track got the bad news when he returned to the barracks that night.

Zulu, Felipe Rodriguez and Antonio Poreso waited for him at the doorway. The expressions on their faces were the first giveaway. Track walked up to them and noted George's absence. He stepped inside the building with the other three following him. Track glanced down the row of sleeping mats. "Where is he?"

"The sweat box," Zulu sadly reported. "He didn't heed your advice, Dan, and completely lost his head when a guard began acting the bully."

A hurried council of war, carried on in whispers, was the first order of business.

Track motioned to his friends. "Let's get down to our area where we can talk."

"An excellent idea, old son," Zulu said. He beckoned for Poreso and Felipe to accompany them.

When they were far enough from the others, Track settled down onto his mat. "Okay," he began. "How long will they leave him in there?"

Poresco shrugged. "It is difficult to tell. If they want for him to die, then he come out dead. For to punish, maybe one or two days."

Zulu was grimly optimistic. "He's a tough lad, our George. He can last out."

But Poreso shook his head. "He is white man. The heat down here is tough for Hispanics, blacks and Indians—for George it is a killer. Believe me—" he pointed to Felipe "—the two of us, we know. I go in there and I don't know how much time go by. The same for Felipe. He spend five days and he think it was five hours. The head go crazy with the heat, man."

"How long has George been in the box?" Track asked.

"He should still be in excellent shape," Zulu said. "They took him away during the late afternoon. He probably had no more than an hour or two of hot sun."

Poreso consulted with Felipe since he was considered the resident expert on the sweat boxes. He turned back to Track and Zulu. "Felipe say that George be okay. Go through hell, but he will get better during the dark. But tomorrow maybe he die."

Track was thoughtful for only a couple of moments. When he spoke, his decisiveness showed. "Okay. The shit hits the fan now. I'm starting the operation."

"Good Lord, Dan!" Zulu exclaimed. "Rashness is certainly not called for here."

Track patted the keys in his pocket. "Rash, hell! I'm cool as cool can be. Operation Shag-Ass goes down tonight!"

Zulu was hopeful. "What's that jangling there?"

Track grinned. "The keys to the kingdom, my friend. Compliments of a very cooperative lady."

"What's first on your agenda, Dan?" Zulu asked.

"I'm waiting until this place closes down for the night, then I'm sneaking over to the armory and getting our weapons," Track said.

"But Dan, old son!" Zulu protested. "Camp Oro does not, as you say, close down for the night."

Track was determined. "Then things are going to get real hairy around here before it's all over. Our choices offer neither the luxury of time nor the comfort of safety."

"Do or die?" Zulu asked.

"Do or die," Track answered.

THE CAMP WAS A COLD ONE.

No fire was allowed, and the bandits supped on unheated tortillas and dried meat. Usually the noise and light restrictions were nonexistent, but the constant disastrous contacts with the paratroopers had begun to change the bandits' way of doing things.

They had been victimized by enough sneak attacks at night to realize that the *paracaidistas-casadores* did not play by the book. The bandits never rested after dark and weren't above exhausting themselves to achieve a victory. The old lethargic days of fighting only when it was convenient were gone forever.

The man called Leone was the leader. His assistant, Chapulin, had spent several weeks working hard with the mayor, Ramirez, in preparing for this latest expedition. This had gone on long before the meeting they'd recently held in the hut at San Pasqual. Even though other villagers knew nothing of the scheme, money and resources had been put to good use. A deal made with gunrunners from the other side of the Andes had been costly, but the result was they were better armed than ever before.

Sturdy llamas, burdened with crates, had arrived with some old M-1 Garand rifles that had been used by the Peruvian army before it had switched over to M-16s. They had been stored in a warehouse where a loose system of bad accounting had made looting the inventory a simple, untraceable matter.

Although numbering no more than three dozen, these sturdy, combat-proved rifles, with the .30-caliber ammunition, had taken the entire wealth of San Pasqual to buy.

The bandits consumed their meal slowly and with a great weariness. They had been traveling through the jungle for a couple of days, leaving their families behind while they established a base of operations for the upcoming confrontations with Colonel Torres's men.

Their plan of action was simple.

Hit and run. Inflict casualties and continue to fight until the advantage slipped away. Then steal back into the blessed jungle and play the paratroopers' own game of camouflage and concealment until other opportunities presented themselves. Men would die, but it was hoped that in the end, after enough of the soldiers had been killed, they would go away.

To simple men like Leone—and his lieutenants Chapulin and Placido—the plan seemed good. They knew nothing of the army's replacement depots nor of the fact that they were heading into direct conflict with a madman's dream of a new empire.

Now, with the darkness complete and the guards posted, the little army, so full of bravery and hope, rolled up in their serapes to sleep.

DAN TRACK STOOD UP IN THE BARRACKS. He could sense Zulu's eyes on him as he waited in the darkness. After listening to the breathing of the sleeping men around him, he walked to the door and listened some more.

The compound was almost completely dark. Only half of the gasoline lanterns were in use, and they cast faint yellowish light over the area. Deep shadows, jutting out from buildings and the surrounding vegetation, lay out across the empty expanse.

Track started to ease out the door, then froze.

A sentry's footsteps, slow and regular, could be heard approaching. The trooper stepped under the long wooden awning that ran the length of the barracks and walked up to the door. Track, his back pressed against the wall, held his breath.

A flashlight danced around carelessly as the man made a quick inspection of the interior. Then, with a click, the beam went off. The soldier walked slowly away to his next checkpoint.

Track waited for a full minute before venturing outside. When he did, he moved slowly and deliberately, controlling his breathing and footsteps. He stuck to the shadows as much as he could. It was obvious that he could not take the shortest route across the compound. There was no cover there, and the moon, while not full, shone brightly enough to betray him to any roving soldier or alert guard up in one of the towers.

Track moved away from the area where the armory was located. He had to get near the mountain where the mine opening was situated. The darkness there was the greatest, and it also gave him a good view of the area.

Several times during the half hour it took him to circle the prison, he had to stop and freeze absolutely still. Twice it was because of guard patrols, but once it was some animal who had wandered under the wire from the jungle. Most likely, Track figured, it was attracted by the odors coming from the cooking and eating area. He didn't know what animal it was, except it snuffed loudly and walked around as if it wasn't afraid of a goddamned thing. When it moved out into the moonlight, Track could see why.

The panther finally got the full scent of many men. Sensing unfamiliar danger, the sleek, tawny animal retreated to its natural habitat.

Track finally circumnavigated Camp Oro. He crouched by the wire next to the area where the sweat boxes were located. Another guard made an appearance on his rounds, then went away.

Track noted that the son of a bitch made no attempt to see how anyone locked up in the murderous devices was doing. After several more moments, Track moved into the punishment area.

He paused at one of the sweat boxes and listened. There was no sound from the interior. It was either empty, or the man inside had given up the ghost.

The next three were equally silent. Then at the fifth, he could hear someone murmuring angrily to himself.

"Hello, George," he whispered.

There was a rustle and a bump. "Dan!" George exclaimed under his breath. "What the hell are you doing out there?"

"I came over to chew on your stupid ass!"

There was a pause. "Yeah—well, shit! I'm sorry, man. I really fucked up."

"How're you doing?"

"This place was hell while the sun was up," George said. "It's not so bad now, except it's stuffy."

Track looked around. The longer he stayed there, the bigger the risk of getting caught. "George, listen. The breakout is going down soon, man. You've got to hang on in there until I can get you out."

"No sweat." Then George chuckled. "That was a dumb-ass thing to say. There'll be plenty of sweat in here."

"I gotta talk fast," Track said. "So listen up. I've got a way to get to our weapons. I'll get my hands on 'em and we'll take it from there. There's inside help."

"The nightclub singer, right?"

"Right," Track said. "We'll get to a car and haul ass. Since this isn't an official prison, we don't have to fear the real authorities once we're out of here. But as long as we're in Torres's operational area we'll have to fight."

"I'll hang on."

Track hesitated, then he decided to tell the truth. "Felipe Rodriguez said you could die in there. Don't do it, hear?"

"I hear! I hear!"

"Right on, George," Track said, putting enthusiasm in his voice. "You hang in there until we spring you, huh? No matter how you feel, just remember that we're on our way."

"That'll keep me going, Dan."

"Later, guy. I'm kinda busy now."

"Good luck, Dan," George said. "Don't worry about me."

"Hell, I'm not, Tiger. See you."

But Track was plenty worried.

He left the sweat box area and crossed the open space to the barbed wire. He rolled easily under the bottom strand, then paused to listen for a few moments. When he got to his feet, he hurried silently, efficiently, across to the headquarters building.

A few more careful moments of silent observation told him the area around the armory was empty.

He couldn't have been more wrong.

21

Hessler was humble and grateful. He had expressed his appreciation for being brought directly to Colonel Torres's quarters rather than being interviewed at the guardhouse.

Sergeant Zotol, standing behind the chair on which the little man sat, was impassive. Although armed, he did not conduct himself as a man guarding a prisoner would be expected to.

Torres, standing in front of the prisoner, had not taken that position by accident. With Zotol to the rear, Hessler would be at a psychological disadvantage with a feeling of being hemmed in and carefully watched.

Hessler, though worried, had something else occupying his twisted mind. Pizarro's calendar, in all its golden and jeweled glory, rested on a table set against the far wall. Propped up, the Incan relic brightly reflected the room lights. Hessler's eyes kept wandering over to the treasure. It represented the greatest score of his life, one that would set him up for life, even if he lived to be 110.

"I have reached a decision regarding your status," Torres said.

Hessler, suddenly worried, turned his attention to the army officer. "Yes, *mi coronel*?"

"You are a professional criminal, Don Juan Hessler," Torres said. "And that is a matter of public record, so do not deny it."

"As you wish," Hessler said humbly.

"The papers on you indicate that you have dealt quite extensively in art and other sophisticated loot," Torres said. He smiled in a friendly matter. "You are not a common thug, Hessler. You have real class and a great deal of appreciation for the finer things of life."

"Thank you, *mi coronel*," Hessler said. "I have always prided myself on my taste." He took another glance at the calendar.

"So you have valuable contacts when it comes to disposing of such relics, no?"

Hessler suddenly realized a deal was going to be made with him. He showed some enthusiasm. "*¿Cómo no, mi coronel?* I am able to deal with any item, no matter how expensive or difficult to dispose of."

Torres's smile widened. "That, too, Hessler, is a matter of public record. That is why I've chosen to transact business with you instead of Track. You are a remarkable man."

"Thank you," Hessler said. "What will become of Señor Track?"

"Under the circumstances," Torres said, "I think it best that he be eliminated."

Hessler was doubtful. "Is that possible, *mi coronel*? After all, the American consulate—"

"*¿Ya bastante?*" Torres exclaimed, holding up a restraining hand. "You don't have to worry about the American consulate or any other official snooping around here, Hessler. And that includes Peruvians as well."

Hessler frowned. "I do not understand. How do you—wait! The mines. No one knows of it outside of this jungle, no?"

"You are, indeed, remarkable," Torres said. "But do not bank on being able to blackmail me or work a better deal for yourself. You are at my mercy, no matter where you go."

"Of course, *mi coronel*."

"So, now that you are up-to-date on everything, I shall give you specific instructions."

Hessler leaned forward. "Yes, *mi coronel*?"

"You will leave here and return to Lima," Torres said. "Your assignment will be to make arrangements to dispose of that." He pointed to Pizarro's calendar. "When you have accomplished that task and informed me of the details, I shall have it transported to wherever it must go."

"The National Museum wants it," Hessler explained, "but they can be forced to cough up more money now that Track has been eliminated. You see, *mi coronel*, there is big insurance money involved here. A most lucrative deal can be struck."

"Excellent!" Torres said.

Conversation was interrupted when Ana Garanta walked into the room. She stopped. "*Perdóneme*. I didn't know you were busy."

Torres turned to her. "We will be finished shortly, *mi vida*. Please excuse me."

"Por su puesto," Ana said. She took one look at the bug-eyed little man in the chair, then left. Hessler's mouth hung open in surprise for a few moments before he spoke. "That is Ana Garanta—the nightclub singer."

"Yes," Torres answered. "She's quite popular in Lima."

"I am aware of that, *mi coronel*," Hessler said dryly.

"Ah! Then perhaps you have seen her perform?"

"Several times," Hessler answered. "When I was tailing Track in Lima, he went to her nightclub, too."

Torres suddenly scowled. "Yes?"

Hessler suppressed a laugh. But instead of chuckling, he put on an expression of sympathy and shock. "I don't know how to tell you this, *mi coronel*, except to be brutally frank. Ana Garanta and Dan Track were lovers, *mi coronel*!"

"¡ALTO!" THE GUARD'S FLASHLIGHT BEAM splashed across Track's face. *"¿Qué estás haciendo aquí?"* the man asked in shocked surprise. He reached around awkwardly with his free hand to unsling the submachine gun from his shoulder.

Track's reaction was instantaneous and instinctive. His foot lashed out in a snap kick that sent the offending light spiraling off into the darkness. This was instantly followed up with a *haito* knife-hand blow to the trooper's throat.

The soldier gasped loudly. Track moved in and covered the man's nose and mouth, muffling the sounds until he died. Once he was satisfied there would be no more noise, Track hefted the dead trooper over his shoulder and went into the shadows beside the armory. He continued until he reached the edge of the jungle.

After cautiously moving ten meters into the brush, he slowly lowered the cadaver, then hurried back to the building where the weapons were stored.

On the way, he picked up the still-shining flashlight and turned it off.

Track reached the door. He carefully pulled the ring of keys from his pocket. Slowly, working in the dark, he inserted the first one in the padlock on the door.

The fourth key Track tried, opened it. He slipped inside and shut the door. The armory was windowless, but Track decided to use the flashlight rather than the overhead bulb to avoid any chance of light showing through cracks in the construction.

He swept the beam around and stopped.

The Franchi SPAS-12 assault shotgun, Zulu's Uzi and George's AR-15 were neatly stacked next to the armorer's bench. Hanging on the wall nearby, in proper military fashion were the weapons' bandoliers.

"ANA!" TORRES BELLOWED. "Ana! *Ven aquí!*"

Ana, alarmed, returned to the room. When she saw Torres's pale, agitated face, she knew he had found out about her and Track.

"You have cuckolded me!" Torres yelled. "In my own quarters, you bitch!"

Zotol, knowing that his colonel would want to handle his domestic affairs privately, became the good soldier. "I shall have Track brought up from the barracks, *mi coronel.*"

Ana shrunk back from her former lover's rage, but then Lupita stepped into the room. She had heard the yelling, and had rushed into the bedroom where Torres kept his .45 automatic pistol. The woman held the weapon in her tiny hands, barely able to keep it level.

"Leave my mistress alone!" the little Indian shrieked. She squeezed the trigger. The round went high, plowing into the ceiling and sending bits of adobe plaster cascading down.

Hessler dived behind the sofa as the small woman fired three more times.

Down in the guardhouse, the gunfire drew the attention of the sergeant in charge from his favorite girlie magazine. He shouted the alarm and, following operating procedures, hit the master switch that turned on the searchlights that covered all areas of Camp Oro.

Outside, caught in the brilliant glare, Dan Track froze. Burdened with three weapons and a load of ammo he was unable to move quickly and efficiently.

22

The guards, following their sergeant and the corporal, rushed out into the garrison yard.

One of them spotted Track and yelled. But before any action could be taken, there were more shots inside Colonel Torres's quarters.

This caused a moment's hesitation. A moment was all Track needed.

He swung the SPAS-12 barrel up and on full auto, and zapped out several alternating rounds of solid slugs and buckshot.

The guard detail, a half-dozen men, crumpled under the fusillade. They sprawled on the ground, two of them twitching, while Track backed off.

There was more trouble behind him on the right.

The barracks doors had opened and armed men in various stages of undress had awakened. Well trained and disciplined, what they lacked in proper uniform they made up with the M-16 rifles they packed.

Track cut loose again on full auto and emptied the assault shotgun. Bullets clipped the air around his head and he backed up as he swung the Uzi off his shoulder to use it.

Then Track backed into something solid and his escape was cut off.

Hell was still breaking loose in Torres's quarters. The young Indian woman, Lupita, squeezed off several more rounds. Frightened witless, Ana Garanta ran out the back door of the building.

Torres and Zotol, nervously jumping around in the uneven fusillade that Lupita was hosing around the room, were finally able to react to her attack.

The colonel hit the floor and rolled over to his recliner. He had a backup emergency weapon, a Ruger .22 revolver, stuffed in the side of the chair by the bottom cushion. He pulled it free and rolled over a couple of more times, then raised up on his knee.

Lupita took three rounds in the face before she dropped.

While the Indian woman died, the area outside had turned into a roaring bedlam. Track, with 5.56-millimeter slugs zinging around him, turned to see what the hell was blocking his way out of the exploding arena he was locked into.

He'd bumped ass-end into the Panhard armored personnel carrier.

Firing the Uzi with one hand and holding on to the empty SPAS-12 with the other, Track swept the area in front of him with some quick fire bursts. Then, taking advantage of the lull as his attackers ducked, he pulled open the wide door in the side of the APC and rolled in.

His entrance was instantly marked by the deafening clang of dozens of rounds bouncing off the armored sides of the vehicle. Track crawled forward to the driver's seat. After fumbling for the ignition switch, he found it and fired up the 90-horsepower engine.

Track popped the clutch and felt the four tires dig in. Pressing down on the accelerator, he sped forward, then turned to the gate of the prison compound.

Wooden posts splintered and broken barbed wire twanged loudly when the barrier gave way to the crushing charge of the armored vehicle. Track, peering through the slits, made straight for the barracks.

Within ten seconds, he spun the wheel and braked at the door.

The other prisoners, fearful that a general massacre was taking place, huddled in the barracks. Zulu, Felipe Rodgiguez and Antonio Poreso, on the other hand, had been ready for anything that might occur.

Track worked the door handle and pushed the heavily armored portal open to admit them. Zulu clanged it shut when all were inside. He glanced around incredulously at the mobile fortress.

"I say, Dan! When you plan something, you certainly go about it in a big way."

"I'll explain later," Track said. He'd gone back to the driver's seat. "There's a machine gun in the turret, by the way. Feel free to use it."

"Oh, thanks awfully!" Zulu said with a grin. For a few seconds he scrambled around in the darkness, then found the boxes of linked ammo. After proper insertion and a couple of pulls on the charging handle, 7.62 ammo spewed out, while the APC traveled forward toward the sweat box area.

Antonio Poreso had located the vehicle's toolbox. Knowing they were on their way to rescue George Beegh, he produced the large socket wrench used to change the carrier's tires.

While Zulu threw out more covering fire, Track stopped. Felipe Rodriguez pushed the big door open and Poreso leaped outside, shoved the tool into the hasp and twisted hard. The device gave way and the door opened. George staggered out and was immediately picked up and shoved through the opening. Poreso dived in behind him, and the vehicle roared out again.

By then it was daylight. The pink glow of the rising sun bathed the chaos around them, making it seem unreal. Dead soldier's, hit either by Track earlier or by Zulu's machine gun, were sprawled around the area. Zulu, able to see better than anyone from his vantage point in the turret, suddenly yelled over the noise at Track.

"The woman is behind that building over to the right."

Track turned that way and could see Ana Garanta huddled on the ground. He stepped down harder on the accelerator, driving rapidly over to her.

George pushed the door open. "Let's go!" he yelled.

Ana was frightened beyond all comprehension. She stared dully at them, then closed her eyes and pressed her hands against her ears.

George leaped from the APC. Spurts of dirt kicked up around him as he ran unsteadily across the small expanse to the woman. Still weak from his ordeal in the sweat box, he had a bit of trouble forcing her to go with him.

"¡De jame! De jame!" she screamed, suddenly giving in to hysteria.

George grabbed her arm and pulled. She resisted as he heaved her up to her feet. Suddenly she leaped sideways, then collapsed.

The bullet had hit her temple and blown away half the face so many men had found beautiful.

George let go of her hand. He rushed back to the vehicle.

"There's Hessler!"

George turned and saw the little thief. Hessler was staggering under the weight of Pizarro's calendar. Pure desperation and adrenaline drove him as he struggled up to the

Panhard. When he saw the vehicle was not occupied by soldiers, he stopped. He stared at Track and Company for one incredulous second. "How—"

The volley of shots punched into Pizarro's calendar. Emeralds shattered like shrapnel, turning Hessler's body into a punctured, bloody mess. He screamed in rage, and another flying hail of steel slapped the relic into pieces. The gold hunks scattered around Hessler's feet. Bleeding heavily and in shock, he still held two pieces of the historical object in his hands.

He turned toward the squad of soldiers who had shot him and the calendar into pieces.

"¡Idiotas!" he yelled. *"¡Estúpidos!"*

Then he sat down, his fat cheeks streaked with a mixture of blood and tears. One of the soldiers, who didn't like being called a stupid idiot, raised his rifle and sent the final bullet into the little man's skull.

Hessler toppled over in the midst of the shattered dream.

Track again gunned the engine, and the Panhard sped back through the gate and into a garrison yard. "Somebody get into our bandoliers and reload the SPAS-12!"

"I'll do it, Dan," Zulu volunteered. "By the way, where are we going?"

"To the highway!" Track answered. "This baby can do at least fifty or sixty miles an hour!"

George picked up his AR-15, which Track had left on the floor of the vehicle. He loaded up a magazine and glanced out the rear viewing slit. He caught a last glimpse of Hessler's corpse. The brightening sun glistened off what was left of Pizarro's calendar.

"Damn!" George exclaimed. "The insurance companies are really going to be pissed off about this!"

Track drove through the garrison. A sudden explosion announced that the troopers had brought rocket launchers into the battle.

"Oh, shit!" Track yelled. "Those babies can punch right through this." Then he grinned happily. "Hey, this thing is amphibious."

He bounced out of the camp's road and across the highway. After a short crash through jungle vegetation, they hit the Riachuelo Verde.

Then the motor died.

"What the fuck's the matter with this thing?" George demanded.

Track checked the gauges. "We're out of gas," Track said. "I guess Torres and Zotol were playing with it all day yesterday."

"It's better to run out of gas here than on that highway," Zulu pointed out. "We're moving along with the current instead of sitting still."

"Yes, but we'll be stopped by the shallows up ahead," Track said.

"Then we'll really be up to our necks in shit," George said.

"Look!"

Behind them, as they moved slowly with the current, several boats were being slipped into the water by the paratroopers.

"Hose 'em off, Zulu!"

Zulu cranked the handle and sprayed steel at the pursuers. Then the shooting stopped. "That's it, lads," he said sadly. "Our machine gun is out of ammo."

Felipe Rodriguez, aware of what was going on through Poreso's rapid translations, said something.

Poreso nodded, then turned to the others. "Felipe he say he remember what George say about it to be better to die on your feet than live on your knees."

Felipe said a prayer and crossed himself.

Poreso understood. "Okay. He ready for to die now."

Track left the driver's seat and picked up his assault shotgun. He swung the bandolier of ammo over his shoulder. "We'd all better be ready."

23

The powerless armored personnel carrier drifted slowly with the languid current down the Riachuelo Verde.

Behind it and approaching rapidly, were several squads of Torres's paratroopers in flat-bottomed assault boats. The colonel himself commanded one, while the faithful Sergeant Emiliano Zotol was the ranking man in the other. Two more followed these, making a total of forty men after Track and Company.

Track wasted no time. He popped up over the top of the vehicle's rear bulkhead, pointed the SPAS-12 at the nearest boat and fired a short fireburst on full auto.

The two lead men in the first boat twisted under the hail of pellets and slugs, then rolled out into the water. Within short seconds the river boiled with the attack of hundreds of maddened piranha.

Track tried for another shot, but the APC turned in a lazy circle as it continued to drift. It might have spoiled his shot, but not so for Zulu.

The African stood and aimed quickly before spraying out a fusillade of 9-millimeter slugs from his Uzi. While the Panhard continued its turn, George added to the onslaught.

Five more paratroopers died.

Torres wisely ordered, *"¡Retardan la velocidad!"* The men manning the outboard motors quickly slowed down, allowing more distance to come between them and the drifting armored vehicle.

Zotol was impatient. "*Mi coronel*, allow me the honor of proceeding with the attack."

But Torres shook his head. "No, Sergeant. It will cost too many men. We will be able to deal with this problem when they reach the shallows."

Zotol reined in his exuberance, and obeyed orders.

Back in the armored personnel carrier Track gave his own order. "Save your ammo," he commanded. "They're pulling back."

George wiped at the sweat on his forehead. "I don't know about you two guys, but I'm about out."

Zulu gave his own bad news. "I've only one magazine left, chaps."

Antonio Poreso and Felipe Rodriguez were agitated. After so much time, they were finally out of the prison camp. This brief taste of freedom was so sweet that both knew they would never surrender to the soldiers. Especially with Zotol's telephone and the sweat boxes waiting for them. Both young Hispanics had armed themselves with items taken from the APC's toolbox. Poreso held on to his lug wrench while Felipe brandished a mattock.

After a quiet quarter of an hour—with the soldiers maintaining visual contact only—a grinding noise came from under the floating vehicle, and it came to an abrupt halt.

"Goddammit!" Track swore. "We've hit the shallows."

"Let's get ready, chaps!" Zulu urged them.

Track and Company took up firing positions while Felipe and Poreso made ready to fight it out with the tools in their hands.

A sudden clashing of small-arms fire raked the APC's outer hull. The bullets pinged madly, then sang off into the air. Each time Track or one of his friends tried to raise up, they were forced back down by the steady, efficient firing of the professional soldiers.

George, always the crazy one, managed to leap up and jump away at his trigger until the magazine ran dry. He dropped back to the steel floor. "That's it," he said with an apologetic tone in his voice. "I'm out of ammo."

Track checked his supply. "The same for me. I've got four rounds left."

"Half a magazine here now," Zulu reported.

Poreso brandished the wrench. "We go for to die now!" he said nervously but determined. "Open the big door here on back."

They could hear the shouts of the paratroopers. The soldiers had beached their boats. Torres shouted loudly, *"¡A la ataque!"*

A battle cry came from the troops. Track and his friends could hear the splashing of boots in the shallow water as the attack grew closer.

"Hand to hand!" Track yelled.

Both he and Zulu leaped up, cutting loose with the remainder of their meager supply of ammunition.

Several soldiers in the front rank splashed down into the shallows. But their battle-maddened comrades leaped over their bodies and pressed the assault onward.

Track and Company braced for the collision.

24

Track reached up and pulled the release handle on the large, rear door. It fell open, hitting the water with a loud smack. A large splash of water sprayed out toward the soldiers.

As he leaped out holding the SPAS-12 like a club, Track dully thought it odd that the troopers had ducked to avoid getting wet, yet had charged straight into flying steel to get at the APC.

Track was at the point of a running wedge with Zulu and Felipe to his left, and George and Poreso to his right. Yelling loud in a combination of blood lust and rage, they raced toward the paratroopers.

A fresh salvo of fire echoed from the jungle. A row of troops was mowed down. This was followed by rapid, individual firing from ambush that hit the soldiers like a scythe taking down a row of wheat.

Felipe Rodriguez, catching the sight of his bandit friends in the jungle around them, yelped out, *"¡Arriba! Arriba! Son los hombres de San Pasqual!"*

The little bandits with their large Garand rifles leaped out of the tree line and raced into the midst of the confused survivors of their initial volleys.

Felipe, his eyes wide with excitement, sighted his quarry.

Emiliano Zotol tried to fire off some rounds from his French MAT 49 submachine gun, but he was constrained by bandits and his own men. He slashed wildly with the muzzle, finally getting some room between himself and the others. He started to bring the weapon up for some quick firebursts, but at the sight of the yelling convict in front of him he hesitated in surprise and shock.

Felipe Rodriguez, his eyes open wide and crazed with fury, swung the mattock downward with all his strength. The heavy tine, sharp and pointed, went into the top of the sergeant's skull.

Zotol, blood streaming from his eyes, ears, nose and mouth, reached up and grabbed the handle of the thing stuck in his head. Tough as hell, he didn't die instantly. He staggered backward into deeper water, then collapsed.

His final sensations were of thousands of tiny little teeth ripping the flesh from his bones.

Felipe leaped up and down in a gleeful frenzy.

Track, using *shuto* and *seiken* punches, fought his way through the swirling combat until he reached the point where Colonel Jorge Torres had been forced into a last stand.

The Peruvian officer, his pistol empty, was unable to slam another magazine into the handle. He fought desperately and fiercely against the small men who pressed against him.

Track finally leaped across a short bandit and grabbed Torres. In an effort to remove him from the tangle of fighting men, Track took the colonel's wrist and pulled hard. He twisted and doubled over for a body slam, but both men were perspiring heavily in the heat.

Torres was sailing over Track's head when the American lost his grip. Instead of being slammed to the ground, the colonel continued through the air, landing in waist-deep water.

Torres quickly got to his feet. In desperation he tried to run for the shallows, but the little fish were already ripping into muscles and tendons.

The screams were loud and hideous as he fell. He bounced up and beckoned for help with one skeletal hand that had not a shred of flesh on it. Then he sank into the red water for the final time.

There was a beat of silence, then the sudden reports of rifles followed. The bandits, never ones to take prisoners, finished off what was left of Torres's paratroopers

When the executions were over, Felipe Rodriguez greeted his fellow villagers with manly Hispanic *abrazos*—the male embrace that signified best wished and true friendship. Then he turned to introduce his friends from Camp Oro.

Leone, the bandit leader, grinned widely and shook Track's hand as Felipe gave him the story of what had happened. Leone spoke rapidly to the American.

Poreso, as usual, acted as the translator. "He say he much honored to know you, Dan Track. They come here to attack the soldiers, but find you fighting at them. He think you help much in the fight. He say you stay here. You be damn good *bandido* chief."

Track smiled wearily. He looked a Zulu and George, who stood behind him, then he turned his eyes back to Poreso. "Tell him 'thanks' but 'no thanks.'"

Poreso translated. Leone spoke again. Poreso gestured to Track. "He say that fine. But what about you lead a raid on Rio Vista?"

"I have a better idea," Track said. "Ask him to lay the hell off Rio Vista until the three of us get on the boat there and get the hell out of the Amazon basin."

Again there was conversation between Poreso and Leone. The Mexican shrugged. "He say okay, but you miss a hell of a lot of fun."

"Poreso, just tell the guy that if we have any more fun down here, it's going to kill us," Track said.

George interrupted. "Fun? If we're having so goddamn much fun, how come we ain't laughing?"

Zulu, always the pragmatist, broke off the conversation. "I say, chaps. Let's get a move on, what? We've yet to find out what we can salvage of Pizarro's calendar."

Avoiding the deeper water where the blood-maddened piranha still thrashed, the group of men moved out of the shallows and stepped into the jungle.

EPILOGUE

Sir Abner Chesterton sat in Track's living room sipping the tea that Tassles LaTour, the former burlesque queen who worked as Track's housekeeper, had just served him. He looked out the picture window at the beautiful panorama of New Mexico landscape. A heavy afternoon rain had just ended, and the sun was filtering through the thinning clouds. A rainbow arced across the breathtaking terrain.

Track, Zulu and George were in the room with him. Track and Zulu were none the worse for the mission, but George had suffered a few bouts of dizziness from his time in the box. A medical examination, however, dispelled any fears of permanent or prolonged damage. He just needed some cool weather to put him right.

Sir Abner set the tea down on the coffee table in front of him. "Too bad about Pizarro's calendar. But I'm afraid they weren't able to salvage a thing of historical value."

"Frankly," Track said, "I feel that the freeing of a couple of hundred slaves outweighs any sort of value that damned calendar might have had." Since returning from South America he had sunk back into his mourning of Desiree Goth, and his temperament showed it. "Anyway, the goddamn thing had a curse on it. I'm sure of that. The ancient Incas didn't want anyone to own it, if they couldn't."

George Beegh rubbed his aching temples. "Curse or no curse, at least they can melt the gold down."

"Speaking of gold," Zulu interjected. "What became of the remnants of Torres's outlaw battalion he used to run that mine?"

"The Peruvian military is investigating," Sir Abner said. "Those troops who committed crimes will be punished severely. The innocent men will be parceled out to other army units."

Track stretched his long legs as he slumped on the sofa. "As the old saying goes, 'the wicked are punished, and the righteous rewarded.'"

"Ah, yes!" Sir Abner said. "That reminds me. The Peruvian government will be sending you chaps a rather nice check. It seems there's a reward for the reporting of old Incan gold mines. They belong to the nation, of course, but they're grateful."

"Even if The Consortium is not, eh?" Zulu remarked.

"Now, lads," Sir Abner soothingly, "there's no need to worry about that, is there? That fine organization realizes that the loss of Pizarro's calendar was in no way your fault. And to prove it, The Consortium has another mission for you."

Track looked up. "It doesn't involve historical relics lost in jungles, does it?"

"Not at all, old son," Sir Abner said jovially. "And I shall accompany you on this one as I did when we went to the Caribbean."

"Glad to have your company," Track said sincerely. "What is it we're involved in now?"

"We're going to Japan, actually," Sir Abner said. "There's an experimental farming area there that is covered by one of the insurance companies that belong to The Consortium."

"Farming, eh?" Zulu remarked. "What must we do? Change the weather, Sir Abner?"

"Oh, dear fellow, much more difficult than that," Sir Abner said. "We must put a stop to some rather nasty attacks on the project."

George laughed. "Who're assaulting them? Locusts?"

"Not at all, my boy," Sir Abner said. "As a matter of fact they're having a bit of trouble with renegade ninja."

SB5-R

AVAILABLE NOW!

Following the success of Dirty War comes SuperBolan #5

FLIGHT 741

A routine flight departing Munich for New York is forced to land at Beirut International Airport.

A whispered word echoes through the jumbo's cabin, leaving panic and terror in its wake.

Hijack!

Aboard the giant silver bird the occupants silently await their fate.

And among them is a special passenger. . . .

Available wherever paperbacks are sold or through Gold Eagle Reader Service. In U.S.A.: P.O. Box 1394, 901 Fuhrmann Blvd., Buffalo, New York 14240-1394. In Canada: P.O. Box 2800, Postal Station A, 5170 Yonge Street, Willowdale, Ont. M2N 6J3.